Billie noc... feelings for Zach.

Her secret dampened part of her enthusiasm. Sooner rather than later, she needed to reveal the truth. But she didn't want to risk fracturing the precious relationship she'd developed with Zach over the past few months.

He draped his arm over her shoulders, pulling her closer. "We probably should head back to the yacht before your sister sends out a search party."

"Yes, they can't see us here."

He grinned. "Privacy can be a good thing." He helped her to her feet, and they walked hand in hand back around the rocks toward the small rowboat.

She tipped her face up, desperate to ask the one question smoldering in her mind. "Where does this leave us?"

Narelle Atkins lives in Canberra, Australia, with her husband and children. Her love of romance novels was inspired by her grandmother's extensive collection. After discovering inspirational romances, she decided to write stories of faith and romance. A regular at her local gym, she also enjoys traveling and spending time with family and friends. You can connect with Narelle via her website, narelleatkins.com.

Books by Narelle Atkins

Love Inspired Heartsong Presents

Falling for the Farmer
The Nurse's Perfect Match
The Doctor's Return
Her Tycoon Hero
Winning Over the Heiress
Seaside Proposal

NARELLE ATKINS

Seaside Proposal

HEARTSONG
PRESENTS

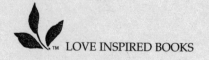 LOVE INSPIRED BOOKS

Recycling programs
for this product may
not exist in your area.

ISBN-13: 978-0-373-48781-3

Seaside Proposal

www.Harlequin.com

Printed in U.S.A.

For the entire law is fulfilled in keeping this
one command: Love your neighbor as yourself.
—*Galatians* 5:14

For my husband, Jay, who encourages me along
every step of my writing journey. I love you.

I appreciate the support I've received
from my dear friends during the writing of this book.
Susan Diane Johnson (Suzie Johnson) and
Stacy Monson, my wonderful critique partners.
I thank my reader friends for their helpful feedback
and support: Jen B, Lisa B, Raylee B, Karinne C,
Tracey H, Daniela M, Heather M,
Jane P and Merlyn S.

Many thanks to my editor, Kathy Davis,
and the team at Harlequin.

Chapter 1

Billie Radcliffe walked barefoot on her timber deck and placed a glass of ice water on the large wooden outdoor table. She inhaled the salty sea breeze, propped her sunglasses on her nose and stared out at the vast expanse of ocean and the golden sand dunes of Sapphire Bay Beach.

The steady pounding of the pristine waves on the shore calmed her overactive mind. She lifted her long dark ponytail off her neck, perspiration clinging to her skin. It was hot enough to swim this afternoon after her sister, Julia, and her new brother-in-law, Sean, returned from their walk in the small township of Sapphire Bay.

During the three weeks since she'd moved into the beach house, Billie felt like she was living in a different universe. A world with a slower pace of life than Sydney. A place where she could relax and ponder the life-changing events of the past few months.

The doorbell chimed and she glanced at the time on her phone. Julia had a key, and her parents weren't due to arrive for a few hours. They had left later this morning than planned and Billie hoped the Christmas Eve traffic on the Princes Highway wouldn't slow their progress on the long drive south from Sydney.

Billie strolled through the spacious living room into the hall and front entrance, the cream floor tiles cool under her feet. She opened the door and her welcoming smile faltered on her lips.

A good-looking guy wearing shorts and a T-shirt stood on her doorstep. His brown hair was cropped short, military style, and he held a small suitcase. A backpack was slung over his broad shoulders, and a late model SUV sat on her drive.

Zach. Julia and Sean's church friend. He didn't look anything like the guy she had imagined.

He held out his hand. "I'm Zach, and you must be Billie." His smile lit up his eyes, an intriguing dark blue with a hint of green reminiscent of the ocean behind her house.

She shook his hand, a tingle of awareness radiating up her bare arm. "Yes, I'm Billie. Please come in." She let go of his hand and stepped back, realizing she'd held on longer than necessary. A smile tugged at her lips and she smoothed down the skirt of her cotton sundress, recovering her composure. "We weren't expecting you until tonight."

"My boss sent us home early." Zach followed her into the living room, leaving his suitcase and bag beside the staircase next to the open plan kitchen.

She grinned and held his warm gaze. "Sounds like my kind of boss."

His eyes sparkled. "He's a good guy."

Billie nodded and headed into the kitchen. "I've made pasta sauce for dinner. Julia and Sean will be back soon, and my parents should be here for dinner." She opened the fridge. "Would you like a drink?"

"Water is fine, thanks." He sat on a stool at the granite-topped island in the center of the modern kitchen.

"No problem." She poured two glasses of water and added ice. Air-conditioning purred in the background, cooling the interior of the house. "Please make yourself at home, and I'll show you to your room upstairs."

"Thanks." He sipped his water. "Have I interrupted your plans for the afternoon?"

"Not at all. The clinic where I work is closed until the New Year. I just finished wrapping all my Christmas presents, and I was going to read out on the deck." A Christmas tree strung with fairy lights and ornaments stood tall in the far corner of the living room. Colorful presents were positioned around the base of the tree.

"Sounds like a nice afternoon." He glanced around the kitchen. "Julia mentioned you're a podiatrist."

"Yes, I'm the feet lady."

He raised an eyebrow. "That's an interesting way to describe your job."

She chuckled. "I'm used to being teased about my job, so now I tell everyone up front and get the awkwardness out of the way."

"I like your attitude."

She gave him a dazzling smile. "I think you can stay this week, now that you've passed the feet test."

"I'm glad to hear it. And you have a great house." He walked over to the sliding glass door, his gaze taking in the beach and ocean. "The view is magnificent."

"I know. I fell in love with this house the first time I saw it, when I visited for my job interview." She sighed. "I'm going to miss living right next to the beach when I move back to Sydney."

"Are you staying long?"

"Two more months. I need to return to my usual job in March when my new apartment is ready."

"I'm only here until February, myself."

"Are you staying in Riverwood?"

He nodded. "In a holiday apartment."

"I commute into Riverwood for work. It's a nice town—much bigger than Sapphire Bay."

"But it doesn't have a beach."

"True." She tipped her head to the side. "Do you work in Riverwood, too?" Julia had mentioned that Zach was a youth worker, and she hadn't asked for further details. As a rule, Billie tried to avoid church people.

"Yes, at Riverwood Community Church."

She nodded, her stomach tightening into a hard ball. At least he didn't appear to recognize her. She didn't want Julia to learn about her visits to Riverwood's church.

Footsteps sounded at the front of the house. Julia and Sean appeared in the living room, holding hands and beaming like they were still on their honeymoon.

"Hey, Zach." Julia gave Zach a brief hug. "Billie, I bought lettuce, although it has probably wilted in the heat." She stowed the bag of lettuce in the fridge and wiped beads of perspiration off her brow. "It looks like it's going to be hot tomorrow for Christmas Day."

Billie smiled. "That's why I live by the beach."

Sean greeted Zach and followed his wife into the kitchen. "I'm going out for a surf soon. Anyone else coming?"

Julia planted a kiss on her husband's cheek. "I'll get changed, and join you on the beach."

"Okay." Sean kissed his wife, embracing her in a gentle hug. "I'll get ready now." He stepped away from Julia, his fingers entwined with hers for a moment before heading upstairs.

Billie rolled her eyes. Were her sister and Sean going to be like this for their entire week-long holiday? They had married less than a month ago, and recently returned from a ten-day honeymoon in Hawaii.

Zach drained his glass. "Well, I probably should get settled. I'm singing carols in Riverwood with the youth group before the Christmas Eve service later this evening."

"Sounds great." Julia turned to Billie. "Mom and Dad are coming with us to church tonight. What are you planning to do?"

Zach drew his brows together. "Isn't Billie going, too?"

She cleared the lump in her throat. He *had* seen her at church. "Um, I don't know—"

"Billie hasn't been to church in years, except for weddings and special occasions," Julia said.

Zach met her gaze, his eyes brimming with questions. "Okay, maybe I was mistaken and Billie has a twin—"

"No, Zach is right." Billie squared her shoulders, preparing for the inevitable interrogation from her sister. "I started going to the morning service at Riverwood a few weeks ago."

Julia's mouth gaped open. "You're kidding. What brought about your change of heart? Are you bored living here by yourself?"

She stood taller, determined to deflect Julia's questions. "No big deal, Jules. It was time, that's all. I thought you'd be happy." She kept her wide smile in place and held her secret close to her heart, not ready to share with her sister the inspiration behind her decision to return to church.

"I'm happy, and Mom and Dad will be happy," Julia said. Fortunately, she changed the subject. "I want to check out the Christmas lights in town before the service at eleven."

"We can do that after dinner," she said. "It only takes twenty minutes to drive into Riverwood. Anyway, I'd better show Zach to his room and let him get organized."

"Good idea," Julia said.

Zach grabbed his bags and followed Billie up the stairs. She led him to a small bedroom at the front of the house, overlooking the national park forest escarpment behind the beach community.

"This is your room. The bathroom is the last door at the end of the hall—you'll be sharing it with my parents."

"Sounds perfect." He smiled, a dimple appearing in his cheek. "Thanks for letting me stay. It beats sleeping in a tent at the camping site for the next week."

"I totally understand. I hate camping, and I have plenty of room. I'll leave you to unpack." She turned to walk away.

"Billie, wait." He moved closer to her. "I'm sorry about earlier. I didn't realize your church attendance was a private thing."

She nodded, meeting his gaze. "It's okay and it's not a big deal. I was going to tell Julia sooner or later." Later more likely than sooner. Her sister was nosy, and would push her to discover the real reason behind her change of heart. She wasn't ready to share her secret with her sister or anyone else.

Zach Montford finished unpacking in his room and wandered downstairs. Billie's home was immaculate, the neutral tones suggesting she'd leased it fully furnished. She had a vibrant energy that wasn't reflected in the decor.

He refilled his glass of water and headed outdoors. Billie lounged back in a deck chair in the shade, her knees bent and a paperback novel resting against her legs.

She looked up, a smile on her lips. "Is everything okay with your room?"

"It's perfect, thanks." He held her gaze, captivated by the warmth in her dark brown eyes. "How's your book?"

"An easy read. I'll probably finish it today."

"Okay." He lowered his body into a wooden deck chair, the ocean view a minor distraction from the beautiful woman beside him. "Are you going for a swim?"

"Soon." Her full lips curved into a cheeky grin. "I'm

having too much fun watching Julia fall off Sean's surf-board."

He squinted, catching sight of Julia and Sean in the water. "I thought Julia hated surfing?"

Billie laughed, her pretty face glowing in the muted sunlight. "Me, too. It won't be long until Sean realizes she has terrible balance and gives up trying to teach her."

Julia knelt on the board and planted one foot on the waxed surface, ready to stand. A rogue wave snuck up behind her, wiping her out.

She giggled. "Oh no. My poor sister isn't having a good run."

"I think it might be a short lesson." Simon, his friend and assistant pastor at Beachside Community Church in Sydney, had attempted to teach Julia and a group from church to surf a few years ago. Julia had quit after one lesson, telling everyone she was never doing it again.

"And it will probably be her last lesson." Her tone was teasing but full of love.

"True, but it's great to see them so happy together."

"They're a cute couple."

"Yep." He couldn't recall Julia or Sean mentioning that Billie was in a relationship. "Do you have plans for next week?"

"Not really. I'll go with the flow, see what I feel like doing. How about you?"

"The mission week is going to be busy."

"When do you start?"

"Lunchtime on Boxing Day. The final event is a rock concert on the beach for New Year's Eve."

"Sounds fun. I think Sean and Julia are performing."

"Yes, and they're also part of the mission team." He sipped his water. "They'll be helping out with a few activities."

"That's right. I remember they were talking about doing something for the kids' programs."

He nodded. "Their help is very much appreciated. You're welcome to come along and join in, if you're looking for something to do."

"Thanks for the offer. I'll keep that in mind, but I'll probably have other things to do."

"Sure." He lounged back in his seat, content to chat with Billie. Her reluctance to become involved in church-related activities piqued his curiosity. What had inspired Billie's renewed interest in attending services at Riverwood Community Church?

Billie stood with the church congregation, joining the choir in singing "Hark the Herald Angels Sing." The tune of the familiar carol washed over her, reminding her of the many years she'd attended Christmas Eve services with her family. Julia and Zach lifted their voices in song beside her and she glanced around the crowded church, feeling trapped in a row near the front.

A number of girls had sent Zach admiring looks, although he seemed oblivious to the female attention. He had left her house straight after dinner and slipped into the spare seat beside her before the service had commenced.

The congregation seemed to be enjoying the carol and she made an effort to sing along. Her mother was delighted to see her in church, having despaired that she'd turned her back on her childhood faith.

Her mom didn't understand that her faith was a private matter between her and God, and she didn't need church. She tried her best to obey the Ten Commandments and live a moral life. She didn't need to waste her valuable time hanging around with hypocrites, who said all the right things on Sundays and did whatever they pleased during the rest of the week.

She wasn't going to pretend to be perfect on Sundays. During university she had dropped out of church for good and now, at the age of twenty-five, she couldn't see how regularly attending church would improve her life.

The song ended and she sat down, listening to the Bible readings about Jesus' birth. The hard seat was uncomfortable against her back and she wriggled, wishing she had a sweater to use as a cushion behind her spine.

Zach turned toward her. "Are you okay?"

She nodded, holding his magnetic gaze for a moment before lowering her lashes. She appreciated the unique scent of his aftershave, and the clean lines of his casual clothes. The fabrics looked expensive and fit him well.

Youth workers must earn more than she realized. He drove a luxury SUV and didn't appear to be short of money. Maybe his parents were wealthy, and he had access to a substantial trust fund?

The service passed quickly. Billie's awareness of Zach, sitting only inches away, intensified.

Why had he captured her interest? She couldn't remember the last time she'd been entranced by a man in such a short space of time. And he was a church person. Unsuitable boyfriend material. She didn't need a boyfriend badgering her to attend a whole bunch of church activities.

She stood to sing the last carol, "O Come, All Ye Faithful." Checking her watch, she was glad to see it was midnight.

She looked forward to waking in the morning and spending Christmas Day with her family and Zach. They were celebrating their first Christmas with Sean as an official member of the family. Her parents were traveling to Europe in February for an extended vacation, and this would be the last big family gathering before their trip.

Her gaze swept over the congregation filing into the center aisle. Senior Pastor Wayne Greenborough didn't appear to be here tonight. She was accustomed to seeing him sitting with his wife at the front and his three teenage sons, who left during the early part of the service to attend the youth activities.

She shuffled into the center aisle behind Julia, who was engrossed in conversation with Sean. They gradually started moving toward the door. She anticipated her escape from the claustrophobic building, which was warm despite numerous ceiling fans running at full speed.

They reached the last row at the back.

Zach cupped her elbow for a brief moment. "Have you met my boss, Wayne?"

She widened her eyes, her pulse racing. So he was here tonight. She didn't feel prepared. "Not yet."

"I'll introduce you in a minute. He's a great guy, and I'm learning a lot from working with him."

"Okay." Her gaze zeroed in on a tall man. His salt-and-pepper brown hair had started receding at the front. He wore a bright smile as he greeted the congregation leaving the church. An elderly couple had ducked in front of her and she'd lost sight of Julia, who was ahead in the line.

Her stomach jitters increased as she drew closer to the man she had obsessed over for the past three months. The reason why she had moved to Sapphire Bay, started attending church services at Riverwood.

In her mind she had imagined their first meeting, wondering if he would recognize her, or think she looked familiar. Did he remember the decision from over twenty-five years ago?

She drew level with him and looked up into his hazel

eyes. Genuine warmth radiated from his face. Maybe he wasn't a hypocrite like the majority of church people.

Zach stood by her side and shook Wayne's hand. "The carol singing went well tonight."

"So I heard." Wayne's gaze skittered back to Billie. "My boys said they had a fun time."

Zach nodded. "Wayne, this is Billie. She is kindly letting me stay with her and her family at Sapphire Bay while I help out at the beach mission."

She curved her mouth into a smile, struggling to hold back a wave of emotion that threatened to bring tears to her eyes. "Hi."

She blinked and shook his hand, liking his warm, firm grip.

"Hi, Billie. It's nice to meet you."

She nodded, her words choking in her throat. Her birth father had spoken her name aloud for the first time.

Chapter 2

Zach moved closer to Billie, aware of her discomfort as they waited in line to exit the church.

Billie's expressive face had flushed crimson when he'd introduced her to Wayne. Her long eyelashes remained lowered, hiding her stunning dark brown eyes.

He frowned. Why was Billie flustered by meeting his boss and mentor?

Wayne's gaze flitted to the next person in line before returning to Zach. "Merry Christmas, and Zach, can we talk before the service tomorrow?"

He nodded. "I'll make sure I'm here early."

"Thanks, see you then." Wayne greeted the man standing behind Zach.

Billie bent her head, her dark, silky hair forming a curtain over her face. She spun away from him, moving into the crowd outside the church entrance.

Zach trailed behind as she darted around groups of people chatting on the lawn, her path lit by bright fluorescent streetlights. She made swift progress in her low heels, her long skirt swirling around her slender legs.

"Billie, wait up."

She paused, worry lines forming between her brows. "I'm sorry. Have you seen Julia or my parents?"

"Julia's over there." He nodded toward a gathering of people by the edge of the car park, next to his SUV.

Julia waved and Billie took off, racing to her sister's side. He quickened his pace, catching up with her when she reached Julia.

Billie gave her sister a hug. "For a moment I thought you'd left without me."

"Mom and Dad are exhausted. I gave them my house key so they could leave straightaway, and Sean walked ahead with them to their car." Julia stifled a yawn, and placed her hand on the door of his SUV. "Zach has a car, remember."

"Oh." She turned toward him and ran her fingers through her hair, flicking long dark strands back off her face. "I'd forgotten you'd driven in earlier."

"That's okay." What was wrong with Billie? Her sudden skittish behavior didn't make sense.

Julia tapped her finger on her chin. "I have an idea. Why don't you drive back with Zach? You'll be more comfortable in his SUV rather than squashed in the back of my car."

Billie met his gaze, her wide eyes containing a new vulnerability that touched his heart.

"Sure, I'll go with Zach."

He smiled. "I was going to detour through town to check out the Christmas light displays, but if you're in a rush to get home—"

"No, that sounds great. I'm too wired to sleep anytime soon, and I can always sleep in late tomorrow."

"You're not coming to church?" Julia asked.

She shrugged, her elegant shoulders displaying a golden tan under the spotlight from the overhead streetlamp. "Two days in a row is pushing it, and I can prepare lunch while you're all at church."

Julia took a few steps back. "All right, we can talk more about this later. Sean's waiting for me at my car. I'm really glad you came tonight."

She nodded. "You'd better go."

"I'll see you both in the morning. Merry Christmas." Julia walked away, crossing over to the next row where her car was parked.

Zach located his keys in his pocket and pressed the button to unlock his door. Billie fell into step beside him, and they strolled around the front of his SUV.

She paused when they reached the passenger door. "Do you know which way to go?"

"The kids at church gave me the scoop."

"Good. We drove around earlier and discovered one street where every single house was decorated with lights."

He opened her door. "Was it James Street?"

"I think so. It's a long street on a hill, and it joins the main road at one of the few sets of traffic lights."

"Yes, that's it. We should be able to see the best light displays and arrive back in Sapphire Bay before one."

A hint of a smile hovered over her full lips. "Sounds fun."

He closed her door and ducked around to the driver's side. He'd known Billie for less than a day and he was already in tune with her moods.

Why did he find Billie intriguing? She was easy to talk to, but he had the strong impression that she wasn't quick to share her deepest thoughts. A distinct air of mystery surrounded her. His curiosity drove him to want to get to know her better, and peel back the layers to discover the real Billie.

He slid behind the wheel, the soft leather seat feeling cool despite the balmy temperature outside.

"Are you comfortable? I can turn up the air-conditioning."

She flipped her long hair over her shoulders. "I'm fine, and this beats Julia's car, no question."

He grinned. "I'm glad you approve."

They drove through the suburban fringe of Riverwood, and talked about the displays in the windows and front yards of the homes. A few cars were still out and about and they cruised behind a family in a station wagon who appeared to know their way around the quiet streets.

"Zach, can we stop and look at this house?"

He pulled over in front of a sprawling modern home on James Street. The large front windows illuminated a detailed nativity scene, a contrast to the Santas, reindeer and giant candy canes in the neighboring houses and gardens.

Billie gazed at the house. "They have a star over the stable and manger. This house is definitely my favorite."

"I agree. Even the donkeys look real."

She sank back in her seat, a wide smile tilting up her lips. "One day I want to have a Christmas lights house."

"Did you consider decorating the beach house?"

She wrinkled her nose. "The garage and drive is too prominent at the front, and hardly anyone walks on the beach behind us."

"Your end of the street is quiet, and the back of your house is a hike from the popular part of the surf beach."

"Yes, I must admit I do like the privacy. But I figured there was no point decorating the house if people won't see it. Plus, there aren't many neighborhood kids around to enjoy it."

"Okay, are you ready to head home?"

She nodded, her gaze warm. "Thanks for indulging my love of Christmas lights."

"You're welcome. It's been fun cruising around Riverwood."

"It's a pretty town." She curled into the seat, looking peaceful.

Zach drove back to the main road in town that led to

the Sapphire Bay turnoff. He stretched out the muscles in
his back, settling in for the twenty-minute drive. The quiet
road followed the river to the ocean.

Billie seemed content to stare out the windshield at the
road ahead. She looked at home in the seat beside him,
and a comfortable silence filled the interior of the SUV.

He inhaled her light floral scent with a hint of citrus.
Her intoxicating presence led his thoughts in a direction
that could only bring him grief.

He shook his head, unable to shift his mind onto a different course. His life was too busy and complicated to con-
template a serious relationship, especially with a woman
who seemed disillusioned with church and faith. The decision he wanted to make next year was hard enough, knowing his parents opposed his potential career change.

But he sensed Billie could do with a friend while living
in her isolated house by the beach. Something had rattled
her tonight at church. He could try to help her deal with
whatever issues were bothering her.

Billie unlocked the front door of her house, the foyer
light illuminating the downstairs area.

Zach followed her inside. It looked like her family had
retired upstairs for the evening.

She slipped off her sandals and headed into the kitchen.
"I'm making tea. Would you like hot tea, or something
else?"

He stood opposite her at the kitchen island. "Are you
having black tea?"

She nodded. "It's my favorite." She filled an electric
stainless steel jug with water. "If you're in, I'll make a pot."

His smile widened. "I'm in."

Her heart skipped a beat, his presence a welcome distraction from the emotional encounter with her birth fa-

ther after church. Somehow she had managed to hold back her tears and keep her composure. Sleep would be elusive unless she stayed up until she was too exhausted to think.

She opened the fridge, and pulled out a carton of milk. "I'm going to sit outside for a while and listen to the ocean. You can join me, if you want to stay up?"

"One cup of tea, and then I'll need some shut-eye. The youth group is performing a Christmas skit during the morning service, and I need to get there early."

"No problem." Billie brewed a pot of tea, and located a matching pair of pastel blue ceramic mugs in a cupboard. "Milk, sugar?"

"Milk, no sugar, thanks."

"Same as me." She filled a small jug with milk, placing it with the teapot infuser and cups on a wooden tray near the sink. "Where did I put my keys?"

"Over there."

Zach pointed to her keys, beside her purse on the granite kitchen counter in her direct line of vision. Maybe she was beginning to feel tired enough for bed.

She opened the sliding door and he carried the tea tray outside, setting it down on a small table between two deck chairs.

A nearly full moon was suspended in the sky above the ocean, lighting up the deck and garden in a silvery glow. She lit a number of citronella lanterns along the edge of the deck, the muted orange haze blending with the moonlight. The tangy scent of citronella infused the light sea breeze, cooling her bare arms.

"I hope you don't mind the citronella." She poured tea into two mugs, and passed one to Zach. "If I don't have the candles burning or wear insect repellant, I get eaten alive by sand flies."

"It doesn't bother me." He added milk to his tea. "The sand flies usually leave me alone."

"You're lucky. What time are you leaving for church?"

"Around nine. I have to organize the props, and ensure enough kids turn up to make the skit work."

"I'll see you at lunch. I'm not planning to surface until after ten." The easiest way to avoid attending church. She was overwhelmed by the idea of seeing Wayne and his family on Christmas Day.

She needed time to process their first meeting and make decisions, including whether or not she wanted to talk with him again. Was she prepared to follow protocol and contact him through formal channels? Did she want to take a risk, and reveal her true identity before she returned to Sydney?

Zach sipped his tea. "This is good."

"Thanks. Your job sounds busy." She poured milk into her cup and sampled her tea, happy the brew was strong.

"At times it is, and the beach mission will be full-on. But, it's nothing like the crazy schedule of my usual job in Sydney."

She lifted a brow. "Do you work for a church in Sydney?"

"Nope. I work for a merchant bank."

"Oh, that makes sense."

"Huh?"

She grinned. "You have a Sydney accent, and I'd wondered how you can afford your SUV."

"A good point. My church salary only covers my basic living expenses. I took two months' leave from my job to come here. I wanted to gain some perspective, and have time away to think about what I want to do with my life."

"You don't like being a merchant banker? I wouldn't mind your nice paycheck."

"The money is good, and I like the fast pace of my job. I'm never bored, and I always have a new challenge."

"I don't understand." She slid back in her chair, cradling her mug between her hands. "Why would you consider giving up a lucrative career that you enjoy?"

"It's complicated." He turned to face the ocean, his strong jaw silhouetted by the orange glow. "Like Julia, I do volunteer youth work at Beachside Community Church. Years of working full throttle have taken a toll. The opportunity in Riverwood arose, and I decided it was time to take a break and do something different."

"Can I be frank?"

He nodded, his gaze sliding back to her face.

"You don't come across as a typical church person."

His eyes widened. "I guess I'll take that as a compliment." He leaned forward in his seat, resting his elbows on his knees. "Out of curiosity, how would you define a typical church person?"

"I don't know." She tightened her grip around her mug. "Maybe someone who says one thing, and does the opposite. They probably have good intentions, but they seem to believe they have the right to sit in judgment on everyone else."

"It sounds like you've been burned."

His gentle words touched a sore spot deep in her heart.

"Yep, more than once." She bit her lip, memories from her teenage years flooding her mind. "I love my sister dearly, but in the past she has been one of the worst offenders. She has mellowed since she met Sean. He has been really good for her in that way."

Zach sipped his tea. "Christians are human, and make mistakes. Saved, but not perfect, is the old saying."

"I get that, and I know what the Bible teaches. I just

haven't seen a lot of Christian love extended to people who don't fit easily into the cozy little church world."

"The Beachside church community has accepted Sean."

"True, but he's older, and he turned his life around before he went to Beachside. I found the hypocrisy much more difficult to stomach when I was younger."

He ran his hand over his cropped hair. "We all mess up over and over again, no matter how hard we try to do the right thing."

"I know that, but I haven't seen many people with a humble attitude." She pressed her lips together, tension radiating through her body. "I've found that people are too busy blaming someone else rather than taking responsibility for their decisions and mistakes. Or, even trying to practice what they preach."

He drained his mug and placed it on the table. "Billie, I wish there was an easy answer. You can't change human nature, and people will continue to let you down. In my experience, not all church people are the way you've described."

"You're not defending their actions?"

He shook his head. "The church is full of imperfect people who do all the things you've mentioned. If you read the gospels, you'll see that Jesus also had a totally different attitude. He often upset the religious people of his day with his radical views."

It was a while since she'd last read one of the four gospels. Maybe it was time to open up her Bible, and examine Zach's perspective on Jesus' life and teachings. "I'll think about it."

He stood. "I'll pray for you. And you know where to find me if you want to talk more."

"Thanks." She held his gaze, appreciating that he chose

to understand her situation rather than become defensive because she dared to question the status quo.

His eyes softened. "I'll see you tomorrow. Or, should I say later today? Merry Christmas."

"Merry Christmas, Zach. I hope the skit goes well."

"Thanks." He walked inside, closing the sliding screen door behind him before heading for the stairs.

She poured a second cup of tea, her thoughts whirling around like the waves crashing on the shore. Was it possible her birth father was a reasonable man like Zach? Would he be willing to acknowledge her existence and accept her as a part of his family? Or was she an embarrassment from his past—the offspring of a secret indiscretion he'd rather forget?

Doubts and fears gripped her mind. If Wayne learned the truth, she was putting herself out there big-time, and risking her hopes and dreams being shattered. She'd lost the opportunity to know her birth mother, and he was the only living biological relative she could locate through the formal search process. Her only connection with her heritage.

Her birth father held all the power if she revealed the truth. Could she trust him to do the right thing?

Chapter 3

Billie placed a dozen potatoes, wrapped in aluminum foil, on hot charcoals in the outdoor grill on her spacious deck. She stretched her arms over her head, loosening the kinks in her shoulders and back. She'd spent the past hour in her kitchen, preparing their seafood Christmas Day lunch.

Last night she'd fallen asleep around two, and woken this morning after everyone had left for church. Her family and Zach were due back soon, and her parents wanted to open Christmas gifts before lunch.

The ocean sparkled in the late morning sunlight, and smoke from the grill swirled in the light breeze. She swiped a few strands of hair off her forehead that had fallen from her ponytail.

Zach opened the screen door and joined her on the deck, looking relaxed in khaki shorts and a T-shirt.

She smiled. "Merry Christmas. How did the skit go?"

"Really well. The kids had fun." He walked toward her, holding an envelope in his hand. "I'm calling my parents while your family exchanges presents, but I wanted to give you a gift. Merry Christmas."

Her pulse raced and she accepted the envelope. "Thanks, but you really didn't need to give me anything." She flipped the envelope open. "Wow, Zach, this is too much." A generous amount was listed on the gift certificate to her favorite store.

"No, it isn't. I'm staying at your house for a week, and I need to contribute something toward food and expenses."

She held his tender gaze, her heart softened by his sweet gesture. "Thank you." She stepped forward and gave him a hug.

He held her close for a moment and she inhaled his distinctive masculine scent, comfortable in his arms.

She sucked in a deep breath. "Okay, now I feel bad because I only have a small gift for you under the tree."

He grinned. "I think the opportunity to stay here is a big gift. Remember, my alternative accommodation is a tent."

Billie wrinkled her nose. "True, and your beach mission starts tomorrow."

"I'll be out of here bright and early to assist with the setup. Is there anything I can do to help with lunch?"

"Not right now. In about an hour I'll need to start cooking the seafood. The salads are made, and I have everything prepped in the kitchen."

"Sounds great. I have a few things to do for tomorrow, and phone calls to make. I should be done in time to help you."

"Thanks." She checked the grill one last time, followed Zach indoors and found his present under the tree.

She smiled and offered his gift. "For you."

"Thank you." He tore the wrapping paper, revealing a baseball cap with a Sapphire Bay logo on the front. "I like it."

"I figured most guys like blue."

His eyes sparkled. "A good guess. I'll be back downstairs soon."

He headed upstairs and she stood beside the Christmas tree. Her parents had added a couple of large presents under the tree this morning.

What were Wayne and his family doing today? She held a delicate glass angel ornament in her hand. Did they open presents first thing in the morning, when the boys woke? Were they having a small family gathering, or a large party with extended family and friends?

She realigned a string of lights that had fallen loose between the tree branches. Did they invite members of the congregation to lunch, who were alone and had no family to share their Christmas Day?

Her thoughts turned to her birth mother and she bit hard on her lip, holding back the tears threatening to form in her eyes. She had to accept the reality of her current situation, and move on. Her hopes and dreams had been dashed three months ago, and dwelling on her melancholy wasn't productive.

The front door opened and her family piled into the house, bringing loud voices and laughter. During their gift exchange she put aside her sorrow and focused on the blessings in her adopted family. Her parents and sister loved her, and she allowed their genuine affection to act as a balm to soothe her hurting heart. No one could replace her family.

Her seafood lunch was appreciated by her guests. She sat next to Zach at her six-seat outdoor table, the powerful ocean rolling in sets of foaming waves as she munched on Atlantic salmon and king prawns.

Billie cracked open a crab leg and sucked out the flesh, the chili flavor exploding in her mouth.

Zach smiled. "You got the chili just right."

She nodded. "I followed the recipe for a change."

"You'll learn Billie is an excellent cook," Julia said. "You won't starve while you're staying here."

Her cheeks warmed, and she dipped her fingers in a small bowl of water, wiping her clean hands on a napkin. "The Pavlova shells are ready to top for dessert. Would you like dessert now or later?"

Her mother sighed. "I think later would suit me. I already feel full, and I could do with a nap."

Her father nodded. "All that driving yesterday has exhausted me, too. I think I'll rest with your mother, and we can eat your Pavlova later."

"Sure," Billie said. "I feel like I need to walk off my lunch."

Julia smiled. "A good idea. A long walk on the sand works for me."

Sean held his wife's hand. "What about the surfing lesson we had planned for today? You promised me that you'd come out again for another lesson."

Billie lifted her brow. "Jules, don't tell me you caved? I can't believe it, after what I witnessed yesterday."

Her sister shrugged. "He talked me into it, and it's a better option than sitting on the beach all afternoon by myself."

Sean grinned. "I can teach you, too, Billie, if you're interested."

"No, I'm fine, thanks. I'd rather walk on the beach and watch you try to teach my sister to surf."

"Fair enough." Sean turned to Julia. "The conditions are good now."

Julia stood. "Okay, if you can wait for our lunch to settle. I'll clear the table and get changed."

"No, I'll clean up," Billie said, lifting two empty platters off the table. "I wouldn't want you to miss out on a minute of your lesson."

Julia groaned. "You just want another excuse to laugh at me."

She stifled a giggle. "The thought never crossed my mind."

"Yeah, I'm sure it didn't. But, I will prove you wrong." Julia picked up two sauce bottles and headed indoors.

"That's my girl," Sean said, following his wife inside with a stack of serving dishes.

She rolled her eyes. "We'll see how long her enthusiasm lasts."

A contented smile settled on her mother's face. "They're both still in the honeymoon phase."

Billie stood. "I know. I'll put a load of dishes through now, so we'll have clean plates for tonight."

"I'll help you clean up." Zach collected plates and cutlery from the table.

She walked beside Zach into the kitchen. "Do you have plans this afternoon?"

He shook his head. "I wouldn't mind walking to the camping ground to discover how long it will take to get there via the beach."

She started packing the dishwasher. "It may be quicker to walk along the road."

He shrugged. "The beach has a better view."

"True, and the cool breeze off the water is pleasant, too."

Her parents, Julia and Sean headed upstairs, leaving her alone with Zach in the kitchen. Six perfect meringue shells sat on a cooling rack in her oven, ready to be topped with fresh cream and fruit for dessert later.

Zach filled the sink with hot water, washing the larger dishes and stacking them on the drainer.

She switched on the dishwasher. "I was going to get changed and leave soon, if you wanted to walk with me."

"Sure." He emptied the sink. "I'll meet you out the back in five."

She finished tidying the kitchen, pleased with their

lunch. Zach seemed to enjoy spending time with her family, and he had complimented her on her culinary abilities. Did he miss being with his family today?

A nice long walk along the beach with Zach for company and Julia in the water for entertainment, sounded like an enjoyable way to spend Christmas afternoon.

Zach dug his toes into the soft wet sand. Sea water submerged his bare feet as the waves drifted in and out along the shore. He walked beside Billie, sunglasses and his new baseball cap shading his face from the midafternoon sun. After indulging in a delicious lunch, he relished the opportunity to walk a few miles on the beach and swim in the ocean later.

Billie grabbed his arm. "Look, Julia is standing on the surfboard."

Julia stood for five seconds, before squealing and falling into the ocean.

He smiled, liking the feel of Billie's hand on his forearm. "She'll get there, with more practice."

The breeze gusted around them and she used both hands to keep her broad-brimmed straw hat on her head, her sunglasses hiding her eyes. "Do you like to surf?"

He shook his head. "I prefer sailing on the harbor."

"Really?" Her smile widened. "It's been a while since I last went sailing."

"You'll have to come out on my yacht sometime, when we're both back in Sydney."

"Sounds fun." She looked out at the ocean, her pale pink T-shirt and knee-length board shorts protecting her skin from the harsh sun. "Go Julia! She's back on the board again."

Sean paddled on a surfboard beside Julia. She lay facedown on her board, bobbing up and down in the ocean.

"She's tenacious, that's for sure," he said.

"And much braver than me. I'd be thinking about how there could be sharks lurking around me."

"You'd have to be unlucky to see a shark around here."

"Maybe, but it only takes one. They're out there, somewhere past the breaking waves, and it's a long swim back in to shore."

"But a fast swim if you can catch a wave in." A large wave tumbled onto the beach, bringing the cool ocean water only a few inches below his knees and the hem of his board shorts. "You don't need to worry. Sean is an experienced surfer, and there are a couple of other surfers out there, too. They'll all look out for each other."

"I hope so." Billie stepped farther away from him and the ocean. She jumped over the incoming water, her backpack bouncing behind her. "The water is a bit chilly. I'm glad Julia's wearing a wetsuit."

"I've noticed the water temperature seems to be cooler here than Sydney."

She nodded. "I think it depends on the currents. I may swim later, when my lunch has settled in my stomach."

"Thanks again for organizing lunch."

"You're welcome. My family is pretty relaxed on Christmas Day. What does your family normally do?"

"My mother makes a big fuss at Christmas. She's coping with my absence because I attended a big pre-Christmas family gathering the weekend before I moved to Riverwood. That's why I missed Sean and Julia's wedding last month."

"I remember Julia mentioning something about it. Their wedding was lovely."

"So I heard—and saw. Julia showed me their wedding album this morning."

"Their photographer did an excellent job."

He grinned. Vivid images of Billie from the wedding photos lingered in his mind. "I thought the bridesmaids looked stunning."

She dipped her head, color rising in her neck. "Cassie would look great in anything. Have you met her? She looks like a model."

"Yes, Ryan and I go way back, and we used to moor our yachts at the same club."

"Wow, it's a small world."

"I did attend Ryan and Cassie's wedding a few years ago."

"I heard their wedding was very posh."

"It was a fun night."

"I was away." She paused, the waves lapping over her bare feet. "We nearly could have met at two weddings."

He stopped beside her. "Did you know Julia used to work with me?"

"Where? At the bank in the city?"

"Yes, in a different division on the same floor."

"It's interesting that our paths haven't crossed sooner."

He nodded, his gaze drawn to the fluffy clouds hovering on the horizon before returning to the beautiful girl only a few feet away. "I'm happy that we did meet each other, eventually."

"Me, too. Anyway, you haven't told me about your family Christmas Day celebrations."

"My mother cooks a turkey for dinner in the evening, and she goes all out, making all the trimmings."

"I'm not big on turkey. I prefer chicken."

"I agree." Not that he'd tell his mother. She was upset with him for taking leave from his banking job, and moving away over Christmas to work for a church. He'd spoken to her before lunch, and cringed at the censure in her voice as she talked about his family's Christmas Day activities.

He continued walking with Billie on the firm, wet sand. "The only time my parents attend church is Christmas morning, and occasionally on Easter Sunday if they're not away on holidays."

"You didn't grow up in the church?"

He shook his head. "Church wasn't a priority in my family. I became more involved when I was at university."

"That's interesting."

"Why?"

"I stopped going to church regularly while I was at university."

He raised an eyebrow. "You weren't involved with any of the Christian groups on campus?"

"Nope. They didn't appeal to me." Billie moved closer to the rolling surf, dropping her hands into the waves and splashing water over her forearms. "It's getting hot and I'm glad I piled on the sunscreen."

"Me, too. You don't look like you're sunburned."

"I don't usually burn, unlike the rest of my family. Julia always said I must have inherited good genes from my birth parents."

"Was she right?"

"Yep. I inherited my mother's Mediterranean skin tone."

"Do you look like her?"

She shrugged. "I've no idea, and I haven't been able to locate a photo."

"You haven't met her?"

She pressed her lips together, keeping pace with him as they walked on the hard-packed sand. "Back in September I discovered that she'd passed away fifteen years ago."

He drew in a sharp breath. "Billie, I'm so sorry."

"It's okay." She stopped walking, and turned to face him. "I had such high hopes of meeting her, and getting to know her. Julia had a shaky start with her birth mother, but they are keeping in touch."

He nodded. "The news must have come as a shock."

"Yes, it's taken me a while to come to terms with it."

"I'm not surprised."

"Today is the first Christmas Day when I've known for sure that I'll never see her again in this life."

"That's really tough." His heart ached for her.

"It's not easy, but it helps being here, away from Sydney and my normal life. I haven't felt this relaxed in ages."

"I like Sapphire Bay. It's a nice community," he said, thinking of the people he'd met through the church.

"So I've discovered." She frowned. "I also don't know if my birth mother has any family in Australia. Her parents migrated here, and she was born in Sydney. She passed away in Italy after living there for many years. I don't know if her parents moved back to their homeland, or if she has any siblings here or abroad."

"It sounds like you've done a fair bit of research."

"There's still a lot more to do. But it got me thinking more about the afterlife."

He nodded. "Death has a habit of drawing our thoughts in that direction."

"I hope and pray I'll have the opportunity to meet her in heaven."

"It's possible." The missing pieces in the puzzle were coming together. The news about her birth mother's death was the impetus for Billie to reconsider her faith and return to church. *Lord, please help Billie to build a closer relationship with You, as she comes to terms with the harsh realities of her birth mother's passing.*

Chapter 4

A few days later, Zach rounded up a group of young people at their Sapphire Bay campsite and organized two beach volleyball teams. The mission were regulars at this beach after Christmas, and they'd introduced Zach to a number of families in the adjoining campground.

He'd brought his beach volleyball equipment from Sydney, marked the lines in the soft sand with tape and set up the net. A tall row of Norfolk pines shaded the court from the late afternoon sun.

Zach moved into position on the sand and glanced around the beach, hoping to see Billie. They had fallen into a routine of staying up late, relaxing outside in her comfortable deck chairs and talking about their days. He left the beach house early in the morning, often not returning until the sun set around eight-thirty.

Billie spoiled him by setting aside a plate for his dinner each night. He appreciated her cooking, a big improvement on camp food. Last night she'd mentioned she might stop by and visit during her afternoon walk along the beach.

His beach volleyball team, a mix of teen boys and girls, were on top of their game and winning the majority of points. He brushed sand off his arms and legs, his sunglasses protecting his eyes as he dove around the court.

The light breeze cooled his warm skin, the exertion from the energetic game upping his heart rate.

He led his team around the net to the other side of the court and gave Dan, the opposing team captain, a high five.

Dan paused at the net. "What time are we breaking?"

"Four-thirty. Julia is bringing refreshments and dinner will be served after five."

"I heard we're having hot dogs. Are you still doing the talk?"

He nodded. "I hope the microphone is working."

"Yeah, we could have a big crowd tonight. Hot dogs are always popular."

"Okay, we'll see if we can finish this game before we break."

"Good plan."

Dan was doing a great job, as usual. He was a committed member of the team and a youth group leader at Riverwood. It wouldn't surprise Zach if Dan followed in his father Wayne's footsteps.

Zach served the ball deep, scoring an ace in the corner. Dan's younger brother, Josh, gave him a thumbs-up. Josh wanted to beat Dan's team, sibling rivalry alive and well in the Greenborough family. Their youngest brother, Tim, was on Dan's team.

A large group of teen girls watched the game from under the pine trees. The beach volleyball matches were a daily event at four, attracting a few spectators now the sand had cooled down underfoot.

Zach caught the ball and moved into position, ready to serve. This time the ball stayed off the sand, bouncing around their opponents before flying back in Zach's direction.

"Mine." He dived to the left, keeping the ball in play.

Josh spiked it over the net, claiming the victory for Zach's team.

The teens on his team leaped up and down, excited they'd won by a large margin. The girls on the sideline applauded and joined the group of players. They headed over to the refreshments table Julia had set up on the grass beside the court.

Zach kneeled in the sand, rubbing his hand over his head to dislodge fine grains of sand from his hair. A familiar laugh caught his attention.

Billie stood three feet away, a broad smile on her face. "This is why you come back at night covered in sand?"

He grinned. "Do you want to join in? My team is winning by miles."

She shook her head. "Not today. I've seen all your expert moves around the court, and you're definitely not a beginner."

His pulse raced, her compliment warming his heart. "I played on the circuit when I was a junior." How long had she watched the game? Was she planning to stay for a while?

"Really? You didn't want to continue?"

He stood, shaking sand off his T-shirt and shorts. "No, I wanted to focus my attention on my studies and I became more interested in sailing. I found sailing relaxing and easier to fit around my study and work schedule."

"True, and who wouldn't want to spend their weekend out on a yacht on Sydney Harbour?"

"I miss sailing. It's my preferred way to unwind after a fast-paced and stressful week at the office."

"Is your job at Riverwood stressful?"

He shook his head. "It's more like a holiday, and I'm getting paid to do things I've previously done as a volunteer."

"Oh, that sounds like a nice change."

He walked beside her to the refreshments table and selected a bottle of water.

Billie greeted Julia. "You're looking busy."

Julia nodded. "We've had a full day. Do you have plans now?"

Billie shook her head. "I'll wander back to the house soon and start preparing dinner. What time will you and Sean be back?"

"Possibly later than usual because we're doing a big dinner here. Zach, do you know what's planned for tonight?"

"We have free time after dinner and we can probably go back to Billie's house around seven."

Julia smiled. "That works for us. Billie, can you stay and help us with dinner?"

She lifted a brow. "What will I need to do?"

"Serve hot dogs. We need to lay everything out on the tables."

"Sure, I can do that."

He gulped down a large mouthful of refreshing water. "I'm needed back on the court."

Billie nodded. "Good luck. I hope your team wins."

"Thanks, it's looking good." He jogged back to the court, ready to play the second half of the match. The teens were waiting for him, their enthusiasm palpable as they planned their imminent win.

Billie left Julia's side and sat by herself on the grass in the shade. A broad-brimmed hat and sunglasses covered her face and eyes, hiding her thoughts.

Her willingness to stay had surprised him. She'd kept her distance from everyone in church, polite if spoken to but content to be in her own space. He hoped the next few hours would be a positive experience for her, and she'd stay long enough to hear his talk during dinner.

* * *

Billie stretched out her legs, her beach towel spread out over the sparse clumpy grass mixed with sand. She'd watch Zach play beach volleyball for a few more minutes before walking up to the campsite to help Julia.

He looked at ease on the court, encouraging and coaching his younger team members as they continued on their fast track to victory. Zach had been in her thoughts often during the days and she looked forward to spending time with him at night.

He waved in her direction and she saluted, her smile lingering.

Why did he find his church job at Riverwood fulfilling? He talked about his work with enthusiasm and energy, pumped and ready to do it all again the next day.

His team won another point and she stood, glancing at her watch. Time to help Julia with dinner. She wandered over to the campsite where Julia congregated with a small group around the grill.

Julia walked toward her and handed her an apron. "You can help us serve the onions in the production line."

"Okay, whatever you need." She'd keep her sunglasses on to prevent the pungent fumes from stinging her eyes.

Billie spent the next ten minutes setting up their section of the table. She slipped gloves on her hands, her hair secured back off her face and apron on, ready to serve.

A long queue had formed just before five. She scooped small portions of chopped onions on the hot dogs held in front of her as their dinner guests progressed along the line. She chatted with a range of people, all keen to enjoy a traditional-style hot dog. The children in the line kept her entertained, many of them repulsed by the thought of adding onion to their hot dog.

Her stomach rumbled and thoughts of her own dinner at

home clung in her mind. Zach was missing from the line. What was he doing? The beach volleyball game should have finished by now.

Fifteen minutes later she stepped back from the table, the queue gone and her cheeks feeling flushed. "Wow, that line was slightly crazy."

Julia nodded. "We only put on two dinners for visitors, and apparently they're well patronized."

"I can see that."

A man's voice sounded through the microphone speakers. She squinted, catching a glimpse of a small makeshift stage near the beach.

She frowned. "Is that Zach?"

"It sure is."

"What's he doing?"

"I think he's giving a short talk soon while everyone eats their dinner."

"Oh." Billie wrenched off her gloves and crossed her sweaty arms over her chest. What was Zach planning to talk about?

"Jules, do you still need me?"

She shook her head. "I'll help clean up now, and we should be ready to walk back to the beach house after six. Sean is around somewhere. Can you stay and wait for us?"

"Yep."

Her sister's eyes held a mischievous glint. "Why don't you move closer to the stage so you can hear him better?"

She bristled at her sister's teasing tone. "It doesn't matter if I don't hear everything he says."

Julia laughed. "We all know you like him."

"What? I don't know what you're talking about."

"Well, Sean and I have noticed you two have been inseparable when he's not working here."

She shrugged. "We're friends."

"I know. All those late night chats on the moonlit deck overlooking the water. A romantic setting, if you ask me."

Heat rose in her cheeks. "Well, I'm not asking you. You're drawing all the wrong conclusions."

Julia's mouth curved into a big smile. "And you're very defensive, which is unusual. Zach's a good catch, and a large number of the single girls at church have been drooling over him for a long time."

"Why do you think he's single? Is there a reason?"

"You know, I haven't seen Zach this relaxed in years. His banking job is insane, with lots of crazy hours and long days in the office. I suspect he hasn't had time for romance, but it looks like he has found time now. With you."

She dipped her head, not wanting her sister to see her words were hitting close to home. Had she fallen into a holiday romance with Zach, without even trying? They'd known each other less than a week. Was that long enough to really know someone?

She ditched the disposable gloves in the trash. "I'll sit over by the trees. See you soon."

Billie rushed away, her heartbeat accelerating. Her attraction to Zach had intensified in a short space of time. He didn't seem like the type of guy who indulged in casual holiday romances.

She settled on the soft grass under a tree, a little farther back from the crowd gathered near the stage. A young guy introduced Zach and passed over the microphone.

Zach stepped forward, and her gaze zeroed in on him. He had a strong presence and a deep voice she could listen to all day long. A small crowd gathered close to him, hushed and focused as they listened to his story.

She watched him, wide-eyed, fascinated by how he'd embarked on his faith journey while at university. He'd been drawn to explore his faith during the phase when she'd moved in the opposite direction. Why was his experience so different from hers?

She shook her head, puzzled and captivated by his words. Later she'd bring up the subject and ask him the questions that burned in her mind. He seemed content and she wanted to know how he'd achieved that sense of peace in his life.

The next morning, Billie drove into an empty space in the car park at Riverwood Community Church. The Sunday morning service started in ten minutes, and Zach had left her house very early to drive a couple of the youth group leaders back to town for church. Julia and Sean had stayed in Sapphire Bay, organizing a morning activity with the team at the campsite.

Billie sneaked into the back row, hiding in a corner of the building. A few of the regulars said hello, and a couple of her podiatry patients stopped by her row for a quick chat. Her gaze roamed over the congregation, smaller than usual due to the holiday season. Pastor Wayne stood at the front with his wife, chatting with a couple of elderly ladies.

She drew in a deep breath, attempting to relax her tense muscles. The sanctuary had a peaceful air, the morning sunlight casting a soft glow on the wooden interior through the exquisite stained glass windows.

Wayne gave his opening address and the congregation stood for the first song.

Zach ducked into the spare seat beside her, a bright smile lighting up his face. "Hey, I didn't realize you were coming this morning. I could have given you a lift."

"No worries, I made an impulsive decision at the last minute. Plus, you have a carload of boys to cart around." She suspected Wayne's sons were at the beach mission, although she didn't know for sure and she wasn't going to ask Zach. She didn't want to be stuck in a car with her half brothers who didn't know she existed.

"The boys are staying in town for the rest of the day."

"Okay." She switched her attention back to the words of the song, remembering the melody from a few weeks ago. She must be moving into the ranks of regular attender if she recognized the songs from the previous weeks.

Wayne preached on a Bible verse in John, talking about how Jesus described Himself as the way, the truth and the life. An old song from her Sunday school days became stuck in her head, reminding her of her carefree youthful days at church. Before problems and issues had cropped up to challenge her faith. Could she return to those simple days, and not let the injustices she'd witnessed haunt her?

His reflections on the Biblical meaning of truth niggled her conscience. She wasn't being completely honest with Zach or her family, let alone Wayne. The risk of someone else learning the truth about her heritage anytime soon was low, but she still had to live with the consequences of her secret.

Did Wayne really believe what he had said? Did he value truth as highly as he proclaimed? Or would the truth of her existence be too difficult to manage?

The service came to a close and her questions remained unanswered.

Zach turned to her, his gaze expectant. "Would you like to go somewhere for lunch? Or, do you have plans?"

She pressed her lips together, his invitation tempting her to tread in uncharted waters. "That sounds fun, but I've promised Julia I'd bring back something for lunch. You're welcome to join us."

"Sure, are you picking up something here or in Sapphire Bay?"

"I haven't decided. I was thinking about grilling fish

fillets, which I can buy fresh in Sapphire Bay from the store near the beach."

"Great idea." Zach greeted a young guy who appeared by his side.

The dark-haired guy smiled. "I spoke to Dad, and he said he'd find the gear you need for tomorrow and drop us back at the beach after dinner."

"That works well. By the way, have you met Billie?"

"Not yet." He extended his hand. "I'm Dan, and I've seen you around at the beach."

She shook his hand. "Good to meet you. Weren't you playing beach volleyball yesterday?"

Dan nodded. "Zach's team whipped us, and the score was embarrassing. Tomorrow afternoon I'm planning to even up the score. You should come by and watch."

"Yeah, I might do that." Dan seemed like a nice guy, and he looked like he was around eighteen or nineteen.

"Okay, I need to get moving. Mom organized a family lunch since the three of us are back in town for the day. Nice meeting you, Billie."

She smiled. "You too. Good luck beating Zach tomorrow."

"I think I'll need more than luck." He waved and walked away.

Zach grinned. "You should be wishing me good luck."

"Yeah, right." She walked beside him along the aisle and outside into the sunshine. "You might need to give him a lucky break tomorrow."

"Maybe. I can follow you back to Sapphire Bay, now that I don't need to collect stuff from Wayne."

She paused beside her car. "You mean your boss?"

He nodded. "Dan will bring back everything I need tonight."

She inhaled a sharp breath, her brain kicking into top

gear. The pieces in the puzzle fell into place. "I didn't realize Dan was Wayne's son."

"Yes. All three Greenborough boys are part of the mission team. I'm parked on the street— I'll wait for you to drive by."

"Sure." She beeped open her car. "See you soon."

He walked away and she lowered her body into the driver's seat, her pulse galloping. She'd been talking to her half brother without being aware of his true identity. And she'd liked meeting him.

Billie fired up the engine, her mind attempting to process her jumbled thoughts. Dan behaved like he came from a good family and he spoke well of his father. Maybe it was time to spend more time with Wayne, and see if he lived up to her first impression.

Chapter 5

Later in the evening, Billie refilled her teapot and carried it outside to the deck. Zach lounged back in his seat, staring at the turbulent ocean. A nearly full moon lit up the cloudless sky, the Southern Cross star constellation was vibrant.

She topped up their mugs of hot tea and passed over Zach's cup.

He smiled. "Thanks."

"You're welcome. I hope it's strong enough."

He sipped his tea. "It's perfect."

Billie settled in her cushioned deck chair, cradling her mug between her hands. She'd miss her evening chats with Zach when he moved back to Riverwood on New Year's Day.

Tomorrow was New Year's Eve, when the townfolk of Sapphire Bay put on a beach concert. Zach's church was involved in the organization of the event.

"The light from the moon will be helpful tomorrow night," she said.

"Yep, and the area near the stage at the far end of the beach should be well lit with floodlights. They're expecting a large crowd. Are you still planning to come along?"

"I'm looking forward to celebrating the New Year. But, you'll have to put up with me hanging around with you.

Julia and Sean will be busy with the concert and I won't know anyone else."

He chuckled. "No problem. I'm off duty tomorrow night. The team activities finish up at lunchtime and we're packing up during the afternoon."

"They haven't roped you into doing anything?" She smiled, pleased by the opportunity to spend more time with him.

"Nope. I have a midweek break for a couple of days."

"Enjoy. I'm back at work on the second."

He stretched out his arms over his head, rolling his broad shoulders. "This week has disappeared fast and it's hard to believe the year is almost over."

"I know, it's gone by way too quick." A year ago she'd never have envisaged that she'd be living in a beach house in a seaside town, accidentally chatting with her half brother this morning, torn over revealing her true identity to her birth father and harboring feelings for a man she'd only known for seven days.

"I wonder what next year will bring."

She sipped her tea. "Who knows? Hopefully good things."

"What are your plans for next year, when you move back to Sydney?"

"I was living with Julia until just before her wedding. My new apartment should be ready when I return, and I'll go back to my old job in Manly."

"You took leave to work here?"

"They were really good about it. It's been a great experience to work somewhere different, broaden my horizons." To follow her dream of knowing her birth father—but she couldn't say that to him.

He nodded. "The bank let me take two months of leave

and an old friend of mine is staying in my apartment. The timing worked out well."

"That's helpful. So, you're going back to your banking job."

"I sure am. It's going to be a shock, working long hours in the office after spending so much time outdoors." He gazed out over the ocean.

"Are you looking forward to going back?"

"Yes and no. I'm enjoying my time here, and the change of pace has been refreshing. I feel more rested and relaxed than I have in years. I like having more time to have a life."

"Yeah, I'm liking the solitude of living here and being less busy, in general. Even my job here operates at a more leisurely pace."

"Have you always lived in Sydney?"

She nodded. "My parents still live in my childhood home."

"Same here. I've discovered that you don't realize how stressed you are from your career until you step back and take a break."

"So, what exactly are you doing with the church job?" She pressed him, wanting to know more about him.

"I'm effectively being mentored by Wayne, and learning from him."

She chewed on her lower lip, distracted from her interest in Zach, a multitude of questions running through her mind. "Has he been a pastor for a long time?"

"He went to Bible college in his midtwenties."

"Do you think he's good at his job?"

He nodded. "You can see for yourself at church on Sundays. He leads and takes care of a thriving church community that's close-knit and looks out for each other. Obviously the dynamic is different here than the city, and Riverwood has a strong sense of community."

"That's true. I've noticed that from work. My clients often say hello to me in church and stop for a chat when I see them around town. I rarely see my clients in Sydney away from the clinic."

"They're a friendly bunch for the most part. I helped out with their end-of-year youth activities, and the week in Sapphire Bay is a big part of my job. In January I'll be involved with various youth programs that the church is running during the school holidays. My job at Riverwood ends when school goes back."

"Have you always wanted to do youth work?"

"I guess so. I've been involved with church youth work at Beachside in Sydney for a number of years." He drank his tea, his gaze focused on the ocean. "My frustration in Sydney was my job limiting my involvement. It could be hard to make it back in time for Friday night youth group, and sometimes I got stuck in the office until late."

"That's not fun, having to work Friday nights."

He grimaced. "I could end up working on Saturday mornings, too. Sailing takes up Saturday afternoon, and Sunday is allocated for church activities."

"Wow, your week sounds crazy busy." That explained why he was single, with no time in his schedule for a relationship. "Did you have any downtime at all?"

"You know, that's been my big revelation since moving here. I didn't realize how overcommitted I was in all areas of my life until I took a break and had time to think and reflect."

"I feel the same way, but my usual schedule isn't as jam-packed as yours."

He held her gaze, his eyes intent. "That's why I'm going to make the most of the extra leisure time I have here, before I return to the hectic pace of my usual life in Sydney."

She nodded, new doubts forming in her mind. When

their holiday from their real lives was over, could it be plausible to consider staying in touch in Sydney? Or, was this window in time an anomaly, a pleasant distraction for Zach before returning to the rat race?

Zach leaned back on his elbows, the grainy sand digging into his arms despite the soft beach towel covering the sand on Sapphire Bay Beach. Billie reclined beside him, her head resting on the bunched-up sweater she'd placed over her backpack to create a pillow.

It was New Year's Eve and they were surrounded by people sitting on the sand and listening to a local rock band perform cover music. Bright lighting illuminated the beach and adjoining park. The local police wandered around the beach, chatting with the crowd. The atmosphere was festive, the whole area designated a liquor-free zone.

Julia and Sean were scheduled to perform onstage soon with the Riverwood church band. They'd spent the afternoon rehearsing their contemporary music pieces at Billie's house.

Zach stretched out his legs. "I'm looking forward to hearing the Riverwood group play their set."

Billie smiled. "Sean was so excited to receive the red Gibson Les Paul guitar from Julia for Christmas."

"It's a great guitar and I'm sure he'll play really well tonight. He's an excellent guitarist."

"So I discovered this afternoon, when the band took over my house."

He laughed. "Did you enjoy the show?"

"They sounded great."

The band finished the last song in their set and announced they were taking a short break. The mayor held the microphone, addressing the audience.

A coffee cart was located nearby, keeping the crowd

fed and refreshed. "Would you like a drink? Coffee, tea, a cool drink? Or, something to eat?"

"A tall latte would hit the spot. It's only ten-thirty, and we still have a while to wait until midnight."

"Yes, we need to stay awake for the fireworks. I've heard the display is really good."

Her smile broadened, her eyes gleaming under the soft glow of the overhead lighting. "I love fireworks and I'm really looking forward to it."

"Me, too." He stood. "I'll be back soon with coffee. Do you want to stay here or come with me?"

"I'm happy waiting here, now I've found a comfy position. Thanks for getting me coffee."

"No problem." He weaved his way around the groups congregating on the sand and joined the line for the coffee cart.

Wayne appeared beside him. "Zach, how's it going?"

"Good. We're enjoying the concert."

"So I can see." He tipped his head to the side. "You look like you're on a date with the young lady who recently started coming to our church."

"Yes, her name's Billie, and we are kind of on a date."

He raised an eyebrow. "Kind of?"

"We're becoming good friends and we like spending time together."

"Do you know her well?"

Zach shuffled forward in the line. "Would you believe we only met a week ago? I've known her sister Julia for years through Beachside Community Church, and we used to work together."

"Oh yes, you're talking about the newlyweds. He's a surfer."

"Yep, that's them all right. They're blissfully happy together."

He grinned. "I met them a few days ago. Is Billie also from Sydney?"

"She grew up in a suburb not far from where I live."

"It's a small world."

"It sure is. I've been staying at her beach house since Christmas Eve with Sean and Julia. They decided to spend the week here with us because Billie was already here for the summer."

"She's living in Sapphire Bay?"

"Only for three months." He moved closer to the coffee cart, the line in front of him disappearing fast. "She signed on for a short-term contract in Riverwood."

"Interesting. What type of work does she do?"

"She's a podiatrist."

"Ah, that makes sense. I've heard a couple of the ladies at church talking about her. She sits in the back row and often leaves the service during the last song."

"That sounds like Billie. Is there anything that happens in Riverwood that your group of church ladies don't know about?"

He laughed. "Probably not. They're pretty sharp and they also like your friend Billie."

"She's a nice girl."

"So I've heard. I'm going to make a point of trying to catch up with her before she disappears after the service. She isn't a regular at Beachside?"

He shook his head. "She only recently started attending church again."

Zach stepped forward and placed his coffee order with the barista. Wayne added his order and moved aside with Zach.

Wayne rubbed his hand over his chin. "Okay, can I say something, at the risk of sounding like your father?"

"Shoot." He respected Wayne and valued his opinions.

"I've been very impressed with the work you've done at Riverwood."

"Thank you. I'm glad my contribution has been helpful."

He nodded. "I also believe you'll make an excellent candidate for Bible college at some stage in the future."

"I appreciate your vote of confidence."

"You're welcome, but there's something else you need to consider."

He frowned. "I do think my parents will come around and support my decision, eventually."

"That's not what I'm talking about. It's one thing for your parents to question your career decisions, but a totally different thing for your wife to not fully support your career choices."

Zach widened his eyes. "Whoa, I think you've leaped ahead and drawn a whole lot of conclusions that may never happen."

Wayne shook his head. "It sounds like you and Billie have connected in a short time on a number of levels. Or, have I read the situation the wrong way?"

"No, you're right." He wouldn't argue with Wayne's astute assessment of his relationship with Billie.

"If you go ahead with your plans for Bible college, would Billie one day welcome the idea of becoming a pastor's wife?"

His jaw fell slack. "I have no idea. Obviously, it's not something that has come up in conversation."

"If it is something you really want to do, you'll need to consider this question if you and Billie become a couple. I'll be praying you make wise decisions and consider all the possibilities before leaping into something."

He nodded. "Thanks, but I don't think you have any reason to worry. I have everything under control."

"I used to think that once, when I was a lot younger. Life has a habit of not always working out the way we want."

Zach's name was called by the barista and he collected two cups of coffee. "Okay, I'll think about what you said and I'd better get back to Billie."

Wayne nodded. "Happy New Year, Zach. Have a good night."

"Thanks. I'll see you in a couple of days. Happy New Year." Zach walked back across the beach, a smile tilting up his lips. He'd continue to enjoy a fun evening with Billie and make the most of the time they had together. Before the real world and problems intruded on their lives.

Billie clapped her hands, thrilled with her sister and brother-in-law's performance on the stage. "Wow, I'm so proud of Julia and Sean. You have a group of talented musicians in your church band."

Zach smiled. "We sure do. They've put on a fine performance tonight."

Billie sat up straighter, stretching out her aching back and leg muscles. "Do you feel like a walk? My muscles are starting to cramp up."

"Are you okay?"

She nodded. "I've been lazy, lying around on the beach for too long."

He chuckled. "We can walk along the shore for a bit. The moon is doing a good job of lighting up the beach."

"A great idea." She stood, packed her towel and sweater in her backpack and slung it over her shoulder. "Which direction do you want to walk?"

"I don't mind. The fireworks will be visible from anywhere along the sand."

"A short walk works for me." They'd arranged to meet

Sean and Julia by the stage after the midnight fireworks, and catch a lift home with them.

She sipped the lukewarm dregs of her latte before tossing the cup in the trash. The crowd on the beach thinned out as they walked away from the stage area. The waves rolled into the shore, pushing the seawater over the firm sand.

He stepped closer to her. "The tide is coming in."

"Yep, I think they've predicted another king tide like yesterday." She was thankful the beach house was elevated, well above sea level. Yesterday the high tide had come within twenty feet of her back fence.

The cover band had returned to the stage for their final set leading up to midnight. Music blasted through the still air, bringing a new lightness to her step. The kinks in her back eased, her muscles warm from the exertion of hiking on the dry sand.

They walked in silence, the salty sea spray cooling her body. The humidity in the air added moisture to her skin, the evening warm despite the light breeze.

She paused by the shore, burying her toes in the soft sand, her gaze taking in the shimmering water under the vibrant moon. "The ocean is so pretty, with the moonlight on the water."

He reached for her hand, twining his fingers through hers. "It's a beautiful night. We should head back, now it's getting closer to midnight."

She retraced her steps, her hand comfortable in his grip. "I'm really glad you stayed at my house this week."

"Me, too. I've appreciated your hospitality and cooking."

She grinned. "Do you cook much?"

He shook his head. "Not really. I sleep in my apartment, but I'm rarely home. My mother is my source of a home cooked meal once or twice a week."

"She spoils you."

"Yep. I'm her firstborn and only son. She worries about me working long hours and not taking care of myself."

"She sounds like my mother."

"It was great to see your parents again, and share Christmas with your family."

"They like and respect you. A lot." Her mother had waxed lyrical about Zach and all the good things he did at Beachside church.

He chuckled. "We've crossed paths a few times over the years. But, I'm glad we met now, when we both have the time and opportunity to get to know each other."

They reached the edge of the shadows, a few steps away from the bright floodlit area.

She came to a halt, turning to face him. "I've enjoyed our late night chats on the deck."

He nodded, swiping a wisp of hair out of her eyes. His fingertips trailed along her cheek. "You're so beautiful."

Color rose in her face, his compliment stirring feelings she hadn't experienced in a long time. "Thanks."

Ten, nine, eight… The midnight countdown over the loud speaker system commenced and the mayor declared the New Year had dawned.

Zach tipped up her chin, his eyes softening. "Happy New Year, Billie."

Her pulse raced, her awareness of him escalating. "Happy New Year."

His intense gaze held hers and he lowered his head.

She closed her eyes. His gentle lips lingered over her mouth, his touch sweet and featherlight, enticing her to respond.

Fireworks exploded in the sky above, breaking the moment. She drew back, her lips tingling and longing for more.

He draped his arm around her waist, pulling her close

to his side, his face turned to the sky. "Wow, look at those colors."

"Amazing. I love it." The fireworks in his kiss had blown her mind, like the shooting lights in the sky.

The reality of their kiss started to permeate her mind, igniting her doubts. What was she thinking? She'd let him kiss her tonight, enjoying his brief touch and being held in his strong arms.

How would she feel about the kiss in the morning, when common sense would override her feelings? A loving relationship couldn't grow and flourish without honesty from both parties.

Right now she couldn't embark on a relationship with Zach. She couldn't risk telling him the truth about Wayne.

She stared at the fireworks, trying to shove aside her romantic thoughts and feelings that included him becoming a more permanent part of her life. Zach deserved better. She'd make the most of their time together in Sapphire Bay, but she wasn't the right woman for him.

Chapter 6

Zach spread the flattened palm of his hand on Billie's waist. His impulsive New Year's kiss replayed in his mind as fireworks streaked the sky in myriad bright colors. The deluge of feelings that had accompanied their brief kiss had taken him by surprise.

Billie's eyes sparkled, her chin tipped up as she surveyed the spectacular sky.

"Was it worth staying up?"

She nodded. "Absolutely. I'm impressed."

The sky show ended and Billie stepped away. She pressed her lips together, her gaze uncertain. "We need to find Julia and Sean."

"They're probably looking for us."

She crossed her arms across her body, as if she were cold. "I don't want to keep them waiting."

"Sure, let's go."

She walked in step beside him, her smile faltering and her gaze averted.

He sucked in a deep breath, his hopes fading. Her emotional withdrawal couldn't be more obvious. The mutual spark during their kiss felt so real—had he been mistaken?

He shook his head, logic starting to tick over in his brain. A holiday romance was not something he'd planned for during his time away from Sydney. Wayne's sage advice rattled around in his mind, feeding his doubts.

She quickened her pace. "I can see Julia next to the stage."

He trailed behind, his steps heavy. His decision would be easier if he'd been drawn to one of the girls at church or on the mission team.

Could he avoid an awkward conversation? He still didn't have a firm gauge on her faith. Keeping his relationship with Billie on a friendship level was a wiser and safer option. He wasn't interested in a holiday fling, and she may not want to explore a potential relationship with him.

He slumped his shoulders, her rejection stinging despite his brain telling him it was probably for the best. Her reaction to their kiss suggested that she agreed with his logical conclusions.

The next morning, Billie cleared the breakfast dishes from the outdoor table and started loading the dishwasher.

Julia wandered inside, stifling a yawn and holding a glass of orange juice. "Sean and I are all packed up and ready to go home."

"I'm going to miss you guys."

Her sister quirked her eyebrow. "You'll have Zach around for a while to keep you occupied."

She shrugged. "He's moving back into his apartment in Riverwood today and I return to work tomorrow."

"You can still catch up. Isn't he here for another four weeks?"

"Yes, that's true. Anyway, I'm happy your week in Sapphire Bay worked out well."

Julia grinned. "Sean and I had a lovely break. The beach mission was busy but we enjoyed it."

"You're starting to get the hang of surfing."

"Yes, but I confess I'm losing my enthusiasm."

"Really?" She rinsed a few coffee mugs in the sink. "I thought you were making good progress."

"It's a lot harder than it looks and I really don't think surfing is my thing."

"You don't need to convince me. Have you broken the news to Sean?"

Julia shook her head. "I don't want to hurt his feelings. He has been trying so hard to teach me."

Zach and Sean walked into the kitchen, breaking off an animated discussion to acknowledge Julia and Billie.

Sean grinned at his wife. "Zach has invited us all out on his yacht sometime when he's back in Sydney."

Julia's eyes lit up. "Thanks, Zach. I'm looking forward to it. Billie, you'll come along, won't you?"

Billie met Zach's gaze, unable to ignore the trace of wariness shadowing his expressive eyes. "Sure, if I'm back in Sydney in time."

Zach nodded. "I'll make sure we pick a date in March when all of us are available."

"That works for me." At least he was willing to continue their friendship. Last night had been awkward. She had gone straight to bed after they'd arrived home around twelve-thirty, and she'd kept her distance this morning. She was still trying to process her feelings for Zach, her attraction growing after their romantic midnight kiss.

Julia finished her glass of juice. "We're going to pack up the car now and get an early jump on the traffic. The roads will be busy."

Sean pocketed their car keys. "All right, Jules, let's get moving." He followed his wife upstairs.

Zach leaned back against a counter, looking at home in her kitchen.

She rinsed cutlery in the sink. "What are your plans for today?"

"That depends on you."

She froze, tepid water running over her hands. "What do you mean?"

He reached across the sink, turning off the tap. "Are we okay? You and me."

She drew her brows together. "Yes, of course."

"I apologize if I overstepped your boundaries last night."

She widened her eyes. "It's all good. You didn't do anything that I didn't like or want." The fact that she didn't normally want to kiss a guy she'd only known for a week was beside the point.

"Are you sure?"

She nodded and placed the cutlery in the dishwasher. "I'm glad we've had the opportunity to get to know each other and I hope we can stay in touch."

"Definitely. We could meet for lunch in Riverwood on Saturday? Unless you already have plans. Or, do you have to work all day?"

She shook her head. "Lunch should be fine. I'm usually finished at the clinic by one, if not earlier."

"I can meet you at the clinic."

"Sounds good. Is there anything exciting happening in Riverwood today?"

"Not that I've heard. Most of the stores close for the New Year's Day holiday and everyone heads to the beach."

"I was thinking about making a simple lunch before hitting the beach this afternoon." She paused, seeking out his gaze. "You're welcome to stay, if you don't need to go back to Riverwood earlier?"

He smiled, a tiny dimple appearing in his cheek. "That sounds fun. I've already packed up my gear and I can drive back to my apartment midafternoon."

Her heart skipped a beat, pleased to have the opportunity to spend more time in Zach's company. "Great. I'll make sandwiches for lunch."

"That sounds great."

She switched on the dishwasher, her lips curving up into a smile. She looked forward to getting to know him better, without any pressure to make decisions regarding the future of their relationship.

The following Saturday Billie leaned back in her chair in the paved courtyard of her favorite café, chosen by Zach for their lunch date. The menu was full of tasty dishes with fresh ingredients. She selected the tempura-battered fish of the day with a side of fries and a green salad.

Zach ordered rib eye fillet steak. The attentive waiter scribbled down their choices and retreated indoors.

She sipped her water, her sunglasses propped on her head. The awning from the veranda shaded their table from the sun. "It's good to sit down and relax."

"You've had a busy morning?"

"I didn't have any gaps between appointments. It seems like everyone needed to get their feet attended to now that the office is back open."

"I thought you'd be quiet at this time of year."

She shook her head. "We've gained new clients, temporarily, from the large number of tourists visiting the region. I think they go on holidays and take a closer look at the condition of their feet."

"Interesting. Or, maybe they haven't had time to see a podiatrist while they've been working, and their holiday time provides them with a good opportunity."

"Who knows? It pays my bills, so I'm not complaining. Anyway, how was your morning? Did you end up going fishing out on the bay?"

He nodded. "We didn't do too well, though. The fish

weren't biting but the youth group had a lot of fun out on the water."

"That's good. I love cooking and eating fresh fish, but I'm not a big fan of catching fish." She wrinkled her nose. "Or worse, gutting them."

"It's not a pleasant job." The waiter returned with a jug of iced tea and Zach filled their glasses. "Do you have a busy week coming up?"

She nodded. "The other two podiatrists, who only work a few days a week, are taking annual leave during January to look after their children."

"It's good they can get their leave approved. Many of the women I work with at the bank struggle to arrange time off during school holidays."

"We can cut back on the number of available appointments to suit staffing levels, whereas I assume the corporate world doesn't stop or slow down over summer."

"It's hectic where I work all year round, except for the week between Christmas and New Year."

The waiter arrived with their entrees. She inhaled the tangy aroma of her fish, her taste buds eager to sample her meal. "This looks good."

He nodded. "I've discovered this café does the best steak in town."

"Are you eating out every night?"

He gave her a sheepish grin. "Do you really want to know the answer to that question?"

She lifted a brow. "Oh, you live here five nights a week?"

"No, but you're close. Prepackaged meals that I can heat in the microwave fill my fridge."

She ate a bite of the fish, the delicate flavors pleasing her palate. "This is divine. No wonder you like my cooking when my main competition is frozen dinners."

"Wayne's wife, Kirsty, is a good cook, too. I sometimes have dinner at their house." He sliced off a piece of his steak, revealing a tender pink line. "The chef here always does my steak medium, just the way I like it."

"It looks juicy."

He tasted the meat and nodded. "Perfect. I also have a couple of midweek dinner invitations from church members coming up. You'll be happy to know I won't starve."

"I'm glad they're looking after you."

He chuckled. "I do miss your cooking."

She tipped her head to the side. "Are you fishing for an invitation?"

"Well, I certainly wouldn't say no to one of your delicious home cooked meals."

"All right, I'll start feeding you on the weekend until you return to Sydney."

"You don't have to cook for me."

She smiled. "I want to, and it's more fun cooking for two. Plus, I've learned you're not fussy." His eyes sparkled as she teased him.

"Thanks, Billie." He turned his head, his smile widening. "Speaking of church, Wayne is heading our way."

She stifled a gasp, schooling her features into a neutral expression. "I didn't know he was here."

"He was lunching with a couple of men from church when we arrived, at an inside table. They've probably finished their meal."

"Okay." She drew in a deep breath, her pulse rate accelerating. He probably wanted to say a quick hello. He may not even give her a second look or talk to her.

Wayne stood beside their table. "Hey, Zach." His gaze rested upon her, his hazel eyes full of genuine warmth. "And Billie, right?"

She pasted a smile on her face, surprised he remembered her name. "Yes, hi. We met briefly at the Christmas Eve service."

"I remember."

Zach nodded. "How's your day going?"

"I just finished lunch with a couple of friends and I saw you both out here. I thought I'd stop by for a chat, if that's okay?"

"Sure." Zach stood. "I'll grab a chair for you." He picked up a spare chair at an empty table and placed it between him and Billie.

"Thank you, Zach. I don't want to interrupt your lunch."

Zach returned to his seat. "It's no problem at all."

Wayne switched his attention to Billie. "I was hoping we'd have an opportunity to talk."

She held his gaze. "Really?"

Wayne nodded. "I've seen you at Riverwood over the last month, but you tend to leave the service straightaway. I like to touch base with new people."

She relaxed her hand, clenched tight in a fist in her lap, and flexed her fingers. "Sure. I know a couple of people in your congregation from work."

"Yes, I heard you're a podiatrist and working here for a few months."

"The timing worked well because I'm between apartments in Sydney."

Zach continued to eat his steak and fries, taking a backseat in the conversation.

Wayne leaned forward in his chair, his gaze remaining fixed on her. "What inspired you to pick Riverwood and Sapphire Bay?"

She almost choked on her mouthful of fish, inciting a coughing fit. She held a napkin to her mouth, attempting to recover her composure.

Zach frowned. "Are you okay?"

"A drink of water might help," Wayne said.

She nodded. "I'll be all right in a minute." She calmed her breathing, her conscience pricking her heart with tiny razor blades. Why hadn't she thought to preplan her answers to the obvious questions Wayne might ask?

Zach turned to Wayne. "Is there anything extra I need to do for the service tomorrow?"

Wayne shook his head. "It's all in the email I sent you yesterday and we have the kids' spot during the service covered. Billie, are you all right now?"

She nodded. "Sorry about that."

"No need to apologize, these things happen. Anyway, getting back to our conversation, what inspired you to live and work here?"

"I love the beach. The house I'm renting in Sapphire Bay is amazing, and my back fence borders the beach."

"Wow. You're living in one of those big houses all by yourself?"

"My family visited over Christmas, and there was enough accommodation to comfortably fit all of them plus Zach."

"Yes," Zach said. "It makes my holiday apartment in town seem tiny by comparison."

"It works for me, and I'm enjoying the peace and seclusion."

Wayne leaned back in his seat. "When are you leaving us?"

"At the end of next month. My parents will be overseas and I can stay in their empty house if my new apartment isn't ready in time."

"I hear you live near Zach in Sydney."

She nodded. "My sister and parents have known Zach for years."

"I know you're not here for much longer, but please let

me know if you want to connect with any of the groups or resources at Riverwood."

"I will. Thanks for the offer but I think I'll pass. I have a few projects I want to work on at the beach house and it's nice to take a break from my usual hectic life in Sydney."

"Don't worry, Wayne," Zach said. "I'll make sure Billie has enough of a social life."

"I've met the neighbors on both sides, who are permanent residents and have retired to Sapphire Bay. We're all catching up for dinner next week at one of our homes."

"Sapphire Bay is a friendly little town," Wayne said. "I wouldn't mind retiring there myself one day. Zach mentioned you're originally from Sydney."

She nodded. "I grew up on the Northern Beaches."

"A beautiful part of Sydney. I haven't been there in years. I think the last time was when my children were small. We caught the Manly ferry from the city and spent the day at Manly Beach."

"The ferry ride is fun."

"I commute to work each day on the ferry," Zach said.

"Lucky you." Wayne smiled. "Billie, he has promised me a day out on his yacht when I next visit Sydney."

"You'll enjoy it." She ate her last mouthful of her delicious lunch, her stomach calming down. Did Wayne plan on spending a lot of time with Zach in Sydney? Another possibility she hadn't considered.

Zach sipped his iced tea. "Wayne, your family is welcome to stay with me in Sydney. I have a three-bedroom apartment and enough space to accommodate you all."

"Thank you, Zach. We'll certainly try and take you up on your kind offer."

Billie dabbed her napkin on her mouth, her web of deception tightening its noose around her neck. What had she done, getting involved with Zach and learning more about her birth father under false pretenses?

She stood, the urge to flee building like an out-of-control fire. "Please excuse me, I need to visit the ladies room."

"No problem," Zach said.

She picked up her purse and strolled away from the table, resisting the urge to run.

The bathroom was empty and she locked herself in a cubicle. She squeezed her eyes shut, blocking the tears that threatened to consume her.

The truth smashed her over the head, her mind reeling from the unwelcome consequences of her actions. She liked him. Wayne seemed like a nice, decent human being. Despite being a pastor, he acted normal and didn't look down on her.

She bit her lower lip hard. How long could she keep up this act before she let something slip? It was possible she could run into him again while she was with Zach.

Lord, I know I don't pray as often as I should. I think I may have misjudged Wayne and totally messed up the whole situation. I don't know what to do, other than avoid him until I return to Sydney. Please help me.

She let out a big sigh. Would Wayne and Zach hate her because of her deception that had seemed logical and reasonable a few months ago? How could she face them at the table, knowing they trusted her? If they knew the truth, would they try to understand why she'd been hesitant to reveal her true identity?

Chapter 7

Zach's gaze followed Billie as she walked back inside the café, her long hair flowing down her back and her purse swinging from her shoulder. She'd seemed a little uncomfortable in Wayne's presence, but he couldn't put his finger on why. Maybe it related to Billie's reluctance to become involved with a church.

Wayne smiled. "Billie seems like a nice girl, and I can understand why you like spending time with her."

"She's a great girl, and lots of fun."

"Have you thought any more about our conversation on New Year's Eve?"

He groaned. "It's complicated and I'm not sure what I'm going to do."

"Relationships are never easy."

He nodded. "I'm praying about it." He couldn't banish Billie from his thoughts, no matter how hard he tried.

"That's a good solution. I was thinking about how different Billie is from her sister. I wouldn't have picked them as being related."

"An astute assessment."

Wayne drew his eyebrows together. "What do you mean?"

"Billie and Julia are adopted."

"Ah, that makes sense. They do look very different from each other."

"Yep. Their parents are long-time members of my church in Sydney."

"So, Billie grew up in a church family?"

He nodded. "It's only in recent years that she's moved away from the church."

"Many young people question their childhood faith in their teens and twenties. That's not unusual."

"I don't doubt she has faith." He rubbed his hand over his hair. "But, you're right. I do question if she'd be prepared to sign up for a life as a pastor's wife."

Wayne nodded and glanced at his watch. "Look, I need to get going. Can you say goodbye to Billie for me?"

"Sure."

"And before I forget, we're organizing a farewell dinner for you at my house on the Monday night before you return to Sydney."

"You don't need to go to the trouble. The Sunday morning tea at church will be fine."

"It's no trouble at all and it won't be a large group." He stood. "I know Billie hasn't been keen on church activities, but she's more than welcome to come to the dinner with you."

"Thanks, I'll talk with her closer to the time."

"Great." He pushed his chair under a nearby table. "You won't need to RSVP for her because we'll have plenty of food."

"Okay, that works for me. I'll see you tomorrow."

Wayne walked indoors and Zach finished his glass of iced tea. Within minutes Billie returned to the table, her eyes bleary and her face flushed.

He frowned. "Are you okay?"

She slipped into her seat opposite him. "I'm feeling a bit tired, that's all."

"Wayne wanted to say goodbye himself, but he had to leave."

She shrugged. "No problem. I probably should go home and do a few things."

"Are you coming to church in the morning?"

She pressed her lips together, her eyes downcast. "I'm not sure, it depends on how I feel. I think I'll catch up on some sleep."

"You could go to bed early?"

"You know I'm a night owl and I rarely fall asleep before midnight."

He smiled. "Why don't you try going to sleep earlier?"

She scrunched her nose. "It doesn't work unless I'm beyond exhausted. Would you like to have lunch tomorrow at my place?"

"What's on the menu?"

"What would you like? I can go food shopping next, if you want to tag along?"

"I think I will. I need to pick up bread and milk."

"The butcher up the road has really good quality meat, most of it sourced locally."

"Okay, let's go."

He finalized their bill and walked with Billie out of the café, ready to hit the stores. She seemed to have gone cold on attending church, for no apparent reason. He'd definitely wait until the last minute before inviting her to his farewell dinner.

Two weeks later, Billie grabbed two bottles of water from her fridge and stashed them in her backpack. It was after two on Sunday afternoon, and she'd shared a pleasant lunch with Zach outside in the shaded part of her deck.

The cool sea breeze had picked up and they'd decided to walk off their lunch on the beach.

Zach came back inside through the front door, his missing sunglasses now sitting on his head. "I found them down the side of my seat."

She chuckled. "You seem to misplace them all the time."

"I have a spare pair in my apartment somewhere, but these are my favorite."

She locked up the beach house and stood beside Zach on the deck. "Which way do you want to walk?"

"We could climb up to the top of the headland. Have you seen the view over the river and bay?"

She shook her head. "I haven't explored that section of the beach. Let's go."

They trekked along the sand toward the township of Sapphire Bay. Sea gulls flew over the pristine water and small fish swam in the waves rolling into the shore.

She dug her toes into the sand. "At least we can walk in bare feet today."

He nodded. "I heard they closed the beach because of bluebottles."

"The sand along the tide line was covered in them. There was no way I was walking near the water's edge." The bluebottles that had populated the beach for the past couple of days had disappeared out to sea with last night's tide.

"Have you been stung by a bluebottle?"

"Yep, when I was a kid. I still remember the excruciating pain. My mother had told me to stay out of the water but, of course, I knew better and wouldn't listen."

He laughed. "Do you ever listen?"

"Sometimes." She smiled, memories of her childhood filling her mind. "I was headstrong when I was younger.

You couldn't tell me anything and I used to get into so much trouble."

"I can imagine."

"Julia was the good girl who always did what she was told. I made up my own mind and sometimes it didn't work out too well." Like her decision to keep her true identity a secret from Wayne. Guilt simmered inside her. How would Zach react if he learned the truth? Would he forgive her?

"I can see Julia playing that role, too."

"She frustrated me because she couldn't understand why I wasn't obsessed with following the rules all the time."

"That's a trait I like in you."

"Seriously? My parents also found that particular trait painful."

"They're your parents and they'd prefer you do things their way."

"That sums it up. I've always questioned the status quo and not been happy to just accept things."

"Has this included questioning your faith?"

"Sort of. I've always believed in God and I probably know my Bible better than you realize."

"You were brought up in the church, so that makes sense, but do you believe what the Bible teaches us?"

"Yes, I do. To be honest, I just don't like people using religion to further their own agendas. Or, pretending to be a certain way to get what they want."

"This is one of your issues with the church?"

"Yep. I know what the Bible says about loving your neighbor as yourself. But, I don't remember seeing a lot of sincere love among church people."

"That's disappointing."

She shrugged. "It is what it is. I can't change the past."

He nodded, staying quiet and keeping his thoughts to himself.

She nibbled her lip, hoping her candid words hadn't offended him. She wasn't going to pretend that she was fully comfortable in a church environment.

They reached the busiest section of the beach where a pair of red-and-yellow flags marked the patrolled swimming area. Her gaze was drawn to her favorite café and ice cream parlor close to the beach.

Zach paused. "Is it that time?"

She pulled her hat lower over her face. "How did you know I feel like ice cream?"

"An easy guess because you always feel like ice cream."

"It's not fair. They have the best gelato that I can't resist."

"It's only a temporary temptation."

"True. I'll return to Manly, only to be tempted by the numerous ice cream parlors on The Corso."

"Beaches and ice cream go together."

She curved her mouth into a wide smile. "They sure do."

They walked up the stairs to the café overlooking the beach. Billie headed straight over to the ice cream counter and the owner greeted her by name.

"Hey, John. Are you having a busy day?" she asked.

John nodded. "The sun's out and the beach is open, what more can I ask? What can I do for you both today? Your usual combo, Billie?"

Zach grinned. "How often do you stop by for ice cream?"

"My lips are sealed," John said. "I look after my customers well and they keep coming back."

She giggled. "I quite like eating a waffle cone while walking home along the sand. I justify the calories by the long walk. It's worth it."

"She's a good girl, doing all that walking every day," John said. "She deserves her ice cream treats."

Zach laughed. "Fair enough. What flavors do you want today?"

She tapped her fingertip on her chin. "Decisions. I think I'll try something different than my usual chocolate combo and have vanilla with English toffee."

"That sounds good," Zach said. "I think I'll have the same."

"Excellent choices." John filled their waffle cones with two large scoops of ice cream, topping each cone with fresh whipped cream, caramel sauce and a pecan nut.

"Thanks, John." Billie unzipped her backpack.

"No," Zach said. "This is my treat."

She met his warm gaze, her heartbeat picking up speed. "Thank you."

"You're welcome." Zach paid for the ice creams and they wandered back outside.

Billie licked the icy treat. "This is good."

"Better than chocolate?"

"No, just different. I think chocolate will always be my favorite, but I do like to try different combos."

She walked over to the balcony railing, admiring the expansive view of the beach. "I'm going to miss this place when I leave."

He nodded. "I can't believe I'm leaving in just over a week. Where has the time gone?"

"What day are you leaving?"

"Monday. I was planning to stay until the following Wednesday but I need to get back earlier."

"Is everything okay?"

"Yes, my friend who's looking after my apartment will be in Canberra next week. He's a political advisor and it's a parliament sitting week. I want to catch him on Monday before he leaves Sydney."

"He's moving out?"

"Actually, he could be staying a while longer. He tells me he's looking for his own place, but I think he's enjoying being fed and spoilt by my mother too much to move out."

"Your mother's looking after him while you're here?"

"Don't ask. She has a perpetual urge to mother everyone who crosses her path. My friend has a complicated relationship with his own parents and enjoys being taken care of by my mom."

"Okay. Your mom sounds nice."

"I know she'd like you."

"Why?" Billie felt her face warm as she waited for his answer.

"You're not that different from her in many ways. She questions everything and isn't afraid to speak her mind. Anyway, do you have plans for Saturday night? Wayne and his family are organizing my farewell dinner at their home. Wayne said you're welcome to come along, if you're interested?"

Her pleasure from Zach's compliment diminished. "I think I'll give it a miss, if that's okay? I'm sure there's a big enough group of people already going who want to say goodbye to you."

"Yeah, I guess so. But will you come along on Sunday to my last service? They're holding a farewell breakfast beforehand." He looked hopeful.

She sucked in a mouthful of ice cream from inside the cone. "That works for me." A breakfast in the church hall was less intimidating than a dinner in Wayne's home with his family.

They traipsed across the sand, reaching the grassy verge leading up to the headland. Billie grabbed her sandals out of the side pockets of her backpack and slipped them on her feet. They climbed the long sloping hill, the soft grass easier to walk on than dry sand.

Her breathing quickened, the exertion of the climb combined with the warm weather taking its toll. "Now I remember why I haven't done this walk."

He laughed. "It's not for the faint of heart."

"It would be easier to drive."

"But not as fun."

They reached the road and followed it all the way to the end. A small parking lot was located next to a lookout that encompassed three sides of the headland, creating a large semicircular viewing platform.

She walked with Zach around the concrete platform, tucking her hair behind her ears. "Wow. This view is incredible. Why haven't I thought to come up here?"

"Probably because you're too distracted by your regular ice cream stop."

"You're not going to let up on the ice cream jokes, are you?"

He shook his head. "You're fun to tease because you take the bait."

"Hmm, I still have a month of summer left to live in this gorgeous part of the world."

"It's idyllic, isn't it? And very different from Sydney."

"The Northern Beaches are a pleasant part of Sydney, but life is always so busy back home. I can't remember ever feeling this relaxed and centered."

"It's a piece of paradise that I'm going to miss. I'm really glad I had the opportunity to do this job. I've learned a lot."

"I thought you said the job wasn't that different from your volunteer work in Sydney."

"Wayne has given me insights into the operations of a

small church in a country town. It's very different from Beachside, which has a number of paid staff."

"I do like that Riverwood is smaller and has a strong sense of community. People know me at church, even though I've lurked on the fringe and haven't attempted to become involved in any of their activities. I guess my job in town has helped."

"Definitely. I've found Riverwood to be a friendly town that welcomes outsiders."

"I think the population size can make a difference." She stood beside him, her gaze drinking in the miles of ocean reaching out to the far eastern horizon. "I don't feel like I'm lost in the crowd and that's a nice experience."

"Are you planning to return to Beachside?"

"I haven't thought that far ahead. Julia and my parents would be ecstatic but it's something I need to do for me rather than to please other people."

He nodded. "I do wonder how many people attend church because it's expected of them rather than because they really want to be there?"

"I didn't know you were such a skeptic."

"No, that's not the right word. I'm more a realist rather than an idealist."

"Okay, that explains why we get on."

He paused. "What do you mean?"

"If you were blind to people's faults, you'd probably be frustrated by my perceptions and experiences."

"Maybe. But I also just love spending time talking with you, walking on the beach."

Her heart skittered to an irregular beat. "Me too. Your presence has made my time here much more fun."

"I'm glad to hear that."

She gasped. "I didn't realize the mouth of the river was more like a large bay."

He shoved his sunglasses up on his head. "It's a nice spot." He reached into his pocket, retrieving his phone. "Photo time, before I forget."

"A good idea." She removed her hat and sunglasses, stashing them in her backpack and pulling her phone out of a side pocket. She snapped a few photos from different angles, capturing the natural light and rich blue hues of the cloudless sky and water.

"Billie."

She spun around, startled to see his phone pointed at her. "Hey, what are you doing?"

He stared at the phone screen, his smile widening. "Taking a cute photo of you."

She scrunched her nose. "I'm sure I look terrible."

He shook his head. "Take a look for yourself."

She examined the photo, her eyes wide and her hair flying around her face. "My hair is a mess."

"No, your hair is beautiful." He leaned forward, twisting a lock of her hair between his fingers. "Silky smooth."

She held his gaze, his eyes compelling her to draw closer. He stared at her mouth and she stepped away, breaking their connection. Her stomach churned, her secret driving a larger wedge between them.

She sucked in a deep breath, recovering her composure. "You better not be planning to post that photo anywhere online."

His mouth curved into a smile. "You're not a fan of social media?"

"I lurk and stay in the shadows. Who wants the attention?"

"Plenty of people, from what I've seen online. But no, that photo is just for me."

Her heart softened, glad that he valued their relationship and wasn't planning to forget about her when he returned to Sydney. "Well, it's only fair that I have a photo of you."

He narrowed his eyes. "Well, if I can't post yours online, you can't post mine, either."

"I won't." She raised her phone, snapping an impromptu shot. "This one's for me."

The photo came up on the screen and her pulse quickened. His handsome face stared back at her, his grin lopsided and a dimple prominent in his cheek. She resisted the temptation to trace his features on the screen with her fingertip. His hair was too short to get caught in the wind.

"Is it okay?" he asked.

She nodded and passed over the phone.

"I've changed my mind."

"Huh."

His eyes sparkled. "It turned out well so you can share it."

"Nope. Your pic is safe with me." She'd treasure the photo and the brief time they'd shared here. But the real world beckoned, and the dynamics of their relationship would change when they both returned to Sydney.

Zach grinned. "I have a surprise planned for Sunday."

"Really? Will you give me a clue?"

"There's a reason they're doing a farewell breakfast for me instead of something after the service. I'll pick you up early and we'll need to leave church as soon as the service ends."

"Why?"

"We have a time deadline to meet."

"I'm intrigued but I need more clues."

He shook his head. "You'll just have to wait and see, but I know you'll love my surprise. It's my turn to spoil you and thank you for your hospitality."

She smiled. "I can't wait."

Chapter 8

A week later Zach stood beside Billie in Riverwood Community Church. He joined with the congregation to sing the closing song of his last Riverwood Sunday service before returning to Sydney tomorrow.

Billie appeared relaxed, having chatted with a few of the senior ladies at the breakfast prior to the service. She'd peppered him with questions about his surprise during the drive from Sapphire Bay early this morning. He'd answered coyly, knowing it was unlikely she'd guess what awaited her in less than two hours.

The song ended and the congregation remained on their feet. Wayne gave a brief closing address before walking down the aisle to the main entrance.

Zach smiled. "Is it okay if we leave now?"

Billie nodded. "Let's go. The suspense is killing me."

"Not long to wait."

"I'm glad."

They moved into the aisle, ahead of the pack since they were seated only four rows from the back. He'd learned Billie didn't like sitting near the front. They scurried into a short line for the door.

Wayne caught his eye, giving him a warm smile. "Zach, I'm going to miss having you around."

Zach hugged the older man, who'd become his mentor

and valued friend during the past two months. "It's hard to leave, but I have to go back to the real world."

"Don't be a stranger. We're not that far away if you're looking for a weekend escape from the city."

"I'll try to visit sometime, although it's probably easier if you can drive to Sydney for a few days."

Wayne nodded. "I appreciate your open invitation."

Zach glanced at Billie. "We have a big day planned."

Wayne shook Billie's hand. "I hope we'll still be seeing you each week."

She gave Wayne a tentative smile. "I plan to keep coming until I leave at the end of February."

"I'm glad to hear this. Okay, you two go and enjoy your last day together."

"We will." Zach cupped Billie's bare elbow and guided her toward his SUV.

"Are you going to give me any hints?"

"Nope. Are you hungry? We can swing by a drive-through on the highway on the way to our destination."

"Oh, we're driving somewhere long-distance."

"You could say that. We'll be doing a lot of traveling today." He beeped open his SUV. "Our time deadline is firm for reasons you'll discover soon enough. Lunch is a few hours away."

He opened the passenger door and she stepped up into the soft leather seat.

"Zach, I'm happy for us to drive straight through because I'm still full from breakfast."

"Okay." He walked around to the driver's side and leaped into his seat.

She secured her seat belt. "I meant to ask earlier, how did your farewell dinner go last night?"

"It was fun. Around forty people turned up."

"Really? I thought you said it would be a small gathering."

"That was the original plan, but it worked out okay to have a larger group. Wayne's house is great for entertaining, especially in summer when you can be outdoors."

"My absence wouldn't have offended Wayne?"

He shook his head, perplexed by her question. "Not at all."

"That's good." She pressed her lips together and stared out the window. "We're heading south. Are we driving to the Victorian border?"

He laughed. "Not quite. Merimbula is our destination."

She tipped her head to the side. "What's special about Merimbula? You know, I haven't been there or even travelled this far south on the Princes Highway."

"You'll enjoy the scenery. This section of the south coast is stunning and not heavily populated."

He settled back in his seat, content now they'd left Riverwood early enough to ensure they'd arrive in Merimbula in plenty of time. Assuming there were no major delays on the highway.

They chatted during the drive and he realized how much he was going to miss her. Billie had become an important part of his life in a short time.

They took the Merimbula turnoff from the highway and drove through the pretty seaside town.

She twirled a lock of hair around her finger. "Are we there yet?"

"Nearly." Zach turned onto a road that was signposted to the airport, driving on the bridge over Merimbula Lake.

She sat up in her seat. "Are we going to the airport?"

"Yes." He swung the SUV onto a road leading to the hangars. A private jet waited for them on the tarmac. "Do you like flying?"

She gasped. "Is that our plane?"

"It sure is. Do you feel like a relaxing scenic flight with lunch this afternoon?"

Billie placed her hand over her mouth, her gaze taking in the small plane. "Wow, that sounds awesome. How many people does it seat?"

Zach smiled. "Twelve, but we'll have the plane to ourselves."

"How? I mean, who owns the plane? Don't they need it today?"

"A friend of mine is visiting and he offered me the use of the family jet today."

"Who's your friend? Anyone I might know?"

"I can't say. He's also a client and the family wants the location of their hideaway to remain a secret."

"Okay." Someone wanted to avoid the paparazzi. Not that she could blame them for protecting their privacy.

He parked the SUV and she walked with him to the plane.

One of the pilots greeted them on the tarmac. "Welcome aboard. We're on time and scheduled to depart in twenty minutes."

"Thank you," Zach said. "Have the refreshments I ordered arrived?"

"The lunch platters are in the fridge in the galley, as per your instructions, Mr. Montford. The smaller drinks fridge has also been restocked for your use. The weather is clear and I can assure you both that you'll have a comfortable flight."

"Excellent." Zach reached for her hand. "Are you ready?"

She nodded, enjoying the feel of his fingers entwined with hers.

He came to a halt at the bottom of the steps at the front of the Gulfstream jet, allowing her to board the plane first. She climbed the steps, walking inside the cabin into a world of luxury and privilege with cream leather seats, a sofa on one side and a table for two opposite covered by a white linen tablecloth.

Zach joined her in the plane.

Her mouth gaped open, her gaze taking in the opulent fixtures and fittings. "This is a top-of-the-line jet. You could buy ten waterfront mansions in Sydney for the price of this jet."

"Yep. It's impressive and very expensive."

She walked along the aisle, checking out the view of the airport through the round windows. "There's no way I would've guessed we'd be having lunch while cruising in a private jet."

He grinned. "I'm glad you approve. Where would you like to sit for takeoff? The front row?"

"Absolutely." She dropped into a seat beside a window, her body molding into the contours of the soft leather. The pilots boarded the jet and made their way into the cockpit.

Zach sat beside her and stretched out his legs. "I'll organize lunch and refreshments after we take off."

"Thank you. I can't believe I'm sitting in this jet. How long will we be in the air?"

"A few hours. The flight path will take us north over Batemans Bay toward Sydney. Then we'll head west over the Great Dividing Range, before heading back east toward Canberra. We'll fly over the Snowy Mountains and Mount Kosciuszko into the High Country region of Victoria before traveling north back up the east coast to Merimbula."

"Wow. How fast will we be flying? I know these jets can do international trips."

He nodded. "We'll be travelling at a more leisurely pace

and a lower altitude than the commercial jets so we can enjoy the scenery."

"Sounds perfect." She fastened her seat belt, savoring every moment of this incredible fairy tale experience. Ordinary people like her didn't travel anywhere in luxury private jets.

Before long the plane cruised along the runway and they were airborne over the water. The Tasman Sea sparkled in the bright midday sunlight. The blue sky welcomed them, not a cloud in sight, as she peered out the windows.

She relaxed back in her seat, a contented sigh slipping out between her lips. "This is the life. I can't imagine travelling like this."

"It's definitely a different world from the usual chaos of negotiating international airports."

"This makes first class look ordinary."

"I agree." He stood. "Well, you don't have hovering flight attendants at your beck and call like you do in first class. You'll have to put up with my efforts."

She laughed. "I'm sure you'll make an excellent flight attendant. Have you been on this jet before?"

He shook his head. "My friend knew I was taking leave from work to do the Riverwood job. He contacted me a few weeks ago, offering the use of his plane."

"I've done a couple of scenic flights during overseas holidays, but nothing that compares to this."

"My friend lives an interesting life. He was born into wealth and does a lot of philanthropic work while shunning the media spotlight."

"Can you please pass on an enormous thank-you from me to your friend?"

"Absolutely. What would you like to drink? I brought your favorite brand of iced tea."

"That would be perfect, thank you."

"Okay, your lunch will be ready shortly." He disappeared into the galley.

Billie leaned closer to the window. The breathtaking scenery stole her attention, the stunning coastline and river systems flowing from the mountains. She spotted the tourist town of Batemans Bay and the bridge traversing the bay. Cars crawled along the Kings Highway on Clyde Mountain, busy with Sunday traffic heading back to Canberra.

Zach returned to the cabin, holding a large seafood platter. He placed it in the center of the table. "I hope you're in the mood for seafood."

"Always." She slipped into a seat opposite Zach.

"I'll say grace."

"Thank you." She placed her napkin on her lap.

He laced his fingers through hers.

She closed her eyes, distracted by his touch, but forcing her attention to his words.

"Lord, thank you for this wonderful opportunity to share lunch with Billie on this jet. Amen."

"Amen." She opened her eyes, reluctant to let go of his hand. The setting was beyond romantic, like a scene from a movie.

He withdrew his hand, his eyes twinkling. "What are you going to try first?"

"The king prawns and oysters look divine. And the lobster salad, how can I choose?"

He cracked open a crab leg. "My friend assured me this restaurant provides the best and freshest seafood in the region."

"Zach, I don't know what to say. You're spoiling me and I really appreciate all the effort you've put into organizing this."

"You're very welcome. I wanted my last day here with you to be special."

She held his warm gaze. "Well, you've totally blown my mind. Words escape me."

He chuckled. "I never thought I'd see the day when you were speechless."

She sipped her iced tea. "You've done the impossible."

They took their time, enjoying a leisurely lunch while picking at the platter that could serve four people.

She glanced out the window. "That looks like Canberra. I can see Lake Burley Griffin and Parliament House on Capital Hill."

"Keep looking and you should see the snow cap on Mount Kosciuszko."

"There's snow in January?"

"Only patches right at the top. You can hike up there from Thredbo during the summer months."

She picked her phone up off the table, ready to add more photos to her collection. The jet flew over mountainous country, wispy white clouds streaking the sky.

"There it is," he said.

She moved to the other side of the jet, a smile curving up her lips. "There's quite a bit of snow on the high peak."

"They had a good snow season last year followed by a mild spring."

"Do you ski?"

"Not as often as I'd like. If I lived closer, I'd ski all the time."

"Me too." She grinned. "I love skiing at Thredbo and I try to get down there at least once every season." Another shared common interest. She snapped half a dozen photos from different angles.

His eyes softened. "Maybe one day we'll have the opportunity to go skiing together."

Her stomach flipped. "Yes, I'd like that." How was she

going to say goodbye to him this afternoon? She didn't want this remarkable day to end.

Five weeks later, Billie locked the door of her new apartment in Manly and headed for the elevator. The chaos of her box-filled apartment could wait until tomorrow. She'd arrived back in Sydney yesterday, stayed overnight with Julia and Sean and organized the moving truck to deliver everything to her new apartment this morning.

She'd kept in touch with Zach since he'd returned to Sydney and his crazy-busy job. He'd sounded stressed the few times they'd chatted on the phone, and she'd mainly contacted him via text messages. She waited for the elevator, checking she had Zach's favorite pair of sunglasses in her purse. He'd left them at her house on his last day at Riverwood after their incredible scenic flight.

The elevator door opened and she stepped inside, her mouth forming a broad smile. That day now seemed like a dream, as if their time together in Sapphire Bay and Riverwood had happened in a different lifetime.

Zach's luxury waterfront apartment complex was only a short walk from her new apartment. She had a nice view over Manly and the ocean from her balcony, but Zach had uninterrupted one-eighty-degree views of Manly and Sydney Harbour from his prime piece of Sydney real estate.

Billie walked along the tree-lined streets with burnished autumn leaves covering the sidewalk. A light jacket kept the Saturday afternoon sea breeze at bay and she'd pulled her hair back in a casual ponytail. Zach had invited her to visit his place for coffee and she couldn't wait to see him again. It was like a part of her went missing when he left Riverwood and she yearned to reestablish their connection.

She pressed the external buzzer for Zach's apartment and an unfamiliar male voice answered.

"Hi, I'm Billie. Zach's expecting me."

"Yes, I'll let you in."

She pushed open the unlocked door and waited for the elevator in the plush foyer. It must be Zach's friend who had answered the door. Zach had mentioned he was still staying with him, a move-out date pending.

Within minutes she walked along the carpeted hall to Zach's apartment. The door was open and a tall man stood on the threshold, an appreciative glint in his eye.

The man smiled, revealing even white teeth. "Well, look who we have here. It's been a long time, Billie."

She widened her eyes, taking in his designer clothes and high-maintenance hairstyle. "Um, I'm sorry, do I know you?"

He looked her up and down. "You don't remember me? I'm devastated."

She shivered, disconcerted by his blatant appraisal of her appearance. "No, I don't have a clue." She didn't want to get to know him better, either.

Zach appeared behind him, a bright smile on his face. "Billie, it's great to see you."

"You too." She hugged Zach, comfortable and safe in his strong and protective arms.

Zach stepped back and held her gaze. "I see you've met Gus."

"Gus?"

Gus nodded. "You may remember me as Angus?"

"That's right," Zach said. "His dad was a pastor at Beachside around six or seven years ago, before my time."

Her mouth fell slack. "Oh, I remember who you are now." Gus was one of the reasons she had left Beachside and turned her back on her childhood church.

Chapter 9

Billie crossed her arms over her torso. Why did it have to be Gus who was good friends with Zach? The one guy she'd disliked the most at Beachside when she was nineteen years old. Back then she'd been naive enough to believe people who attended church tried to follow the teachings in the Bible.

Zach raised an eyebrow. "Are you coming inside?"

"Yes, of course." She pulled her mouth into a smile, determined not to let Gus's presence ruin her reunion with Zach.

She entered the apartment with Zach, Gus trailing behind. Floor-to-ceiling windows in the living room overlooked a large outdoor entertaining area on the balcony.

"Wow." She stood by the windows, her gaze roaming over the familiar landmarks on Sydney Harbour and the northern foreshore suburbs. "I could spend all day staring at this view."

Zach laughed, staying close by her side. "That's what my mom says, even though she lives on the waterfront in a house overlooking Manly and the ocean beaches."

Gus cleared his throat, making his presence known. "I was going to make some espresso. Would either of you like a cup?"

Zach nodded. "Thanks, that sounds good. Billie, what would you like?"

"I'll have the same."

Gus narrowed his eyes. "Are you sure you don't want a cappuccino or a latte?"

"Gus makes great coffee," Zach said. "He used to work as a barista when he was at university."

"Okay." She tried to ignore Gus's smug smile and not let him rile her up. "A latte would be lovely."

"You're very welcome," Gus said. "Any sugar?"

"No, thank you."

"I'll be back soon." Gus left the living room.

Billie let out a deep breath, returning her attention to Zach. "So, why aren't you out sailing on a Saturday?"

"My yacht's temporarily out of action while I wait for my marine mechanic to undertake some routine maintenance."

"That's frustrating."

He shrugged. "Work has been crazy and I've had a chance to catch up on a few things the past couple of weekends."

"That's good. I have a lot of work to do to get my apartment in order."

"Do you want some help unpacking? I don't have any plans for the rest of today."

"Thanks, that would be helpful. I won't need to bother Sean to help me rearrange some of the heavier furniture."

"You got it." He pointed to the leather sofas positioned around a coffee table. "Please take a seat. Gus shouldn't be too long."

She sat beside Zach on the sofa opposite the windows. "It's going to be strange returning to my job in Manly next week, after three months away."

He lounged back, his arm draped behind her on the top of the sofa cushions. "It took time for me to adapt to the faster pace of life again. And I missed you."

Her heart warmed. "I missed you, too." She slid closer

to him on the sofa, remembering the fun times and long chats they'd shared over the summer.

Gus returned to the living room and placed two mugs on the coffee table in front of Billie and Zach. "I'll be back in a minute with the Tim Tams."

"Thanks," Zach said.

She sat forward in her chair, inhaling the aromatic blend. "This smells good."

"Wait until you taste it. I haven't booted him out because he makes great coffee."

"Hey, I heard that," Gus said, entering the room with a plate of cookies. "I'm working on finding a new place."

She sipped her latte and accepted a Tim Tam, biting into the milk-chocolate-coated treat.

Zach devoured his Tim Tam and drank his coffee.

Gus sank into the sofa closest to her. "Billie, is it Tim Tam Slam time?"

"No, I don't think so."

"But you were so good at it," Gus said.

She wrinkled her nose. "When I was, like, sixteen. I haven't done that in years."

Zach's eyebrows shot up. "Did you two hang out together years ago?"

"Yes, all the time," Gus said.

She frowned. "Kind of. We had a number of mutual friends at church."

Gus bit off the two ends of a Tim Tam and placed one end in his mug, using it as a straw to drink his coffee.

Ugh, he was unbearable. More uncouth than she'd remembered.

Zach laughed. "Mate, you look ridiculous."

Gus licked the melted chocolate off his lips. "It's all good fun, isn't it, Billie?"

She shrugged, refusing to get drawn into his game.

She wasn't interested in indulging Gus in a trip down memory lane.

Zach's phone vibrated on the coffee table and he checked the screen. "Sorry, it's work and I have to take the call."

"Sure," she said.

Gus grinned. "No worries, I can entertain Billie."

"Thanks, I'll be back soon." Zach walked away toward the kitchen.

Billie stifled a groan and sipped her coffee.

"Well, isn't this fun?" Gus lounged back on the sofa. "The two of us, alone together."

She glared at him, fed up with his insinuations. "What do you want?"

"A chance to talk and catch up on old times. I heard your sister recently married. Please pass on my congratulations."

She nodded, remaining silent.

Gus sat forward in his seat. "You're all grown up. I knew you were going to become a beauty."

She tightened her grip on her mug. "I really don't think this conversation is appropriate."

"You have nothing to worry about because you're Zach's girl and I know you're off-limits."

"I'm glad to hear you've developed some kind of conscience since we last met."

"Touché. You're a gorgeous girl and you can't blame a guy for wanting to get to know you."

She narrowed her eyes. "If you don't change the subject, you'll discover I still remember how to slap your face really hard."

He chuckled. "I should have pursued you with more vigor years ago. I like a challenge."

She placed her mug on the coffee table and clenched her fists. "Trust me, you would have been wasting your time."

"Maybe, maybe not. Anyway, you've certainly turned Zach's head. Women have been throwing themselves at him for years and you're the first woman to completely distract him."

"I'm not really comfortable talking with you about my relationship with Zach."

"Mark my words, he has serious intentions toward you, which means you and I will be seeing a lot more of each other."

She sipped her latte, the full implications of his words filling her mind. At some point in time she was going to need to tell Wayne and Zach the truth. Maybe she should plan a trip back to Riverwood with Zach. Over the past month she'd attended services at Riverwood but tried to avoid any contact with Wayne or his family.

Gus finished his coffee and stood. "I have to be somewhere. Can you let Zach know I'll be back either later tonight or tomorrow?"

She stifled a grimace. "Sure." He probably had a date lined up with a deluded woman who thought he was nice and charming.

"It was good to see you again. Catch you later." He winked and left the room.

She slumped back on the sofa, placing her hands over her face. Gus was now a part of her life again, whether she liked it or not.

Zach ended the work call and left his study, anxious to return to Billie who was in his living room with Gus. He'd thought about her a lot over the past five weeks, counting down the days until he'd see her again.

He furrowed his brow, curious to learn more about Billie's previous connection to Gus. She was uncomfortable in Gus's presence, the palpable tension between them taking Zach by surprise. Gus had goaded Billie about their shared history, which was out of character for him, too.

Zach walked into his living room. Billie stood by herself near a window, staring out at the view over Manly Wharf. Her dark glossy ponytail shone in the afternoon sunlight and she cradled her coffee mug in her hands.

"Hey, where's Gus?" he asked.

She looked away, tension radiating from her body. "He said he had to be somewhere, and he'd see you tonight or tomorrow morning."

"Oh, okay." Gus either had a secret date lined up, or he wanted to give Zach space to spend time with Billie. "Did you have a chance to talk with him?"

She nodded, her gaze remaining on his timber floor.

He drew in a deep breath. "What happened between you and Gus?"

She looked up, a hint of pain flashing in her eyes before she hooded her expression. "Do you really want to know?"

"I wouldn't be asking if I didn't."

She nibbled her lower lip. "You may not like what I have to say, or even believe me?"

"Billie." He moved to her side, cupping her chin with his fingertips. "You can trust me. I know you'll be honest and tell me the truth."

She nodded, walking away and wrapping her arms around her lean body. "You know how I said I had some bad experiences with church people when I was younger."

"Yes." He frowned. "Does this have something to do with Gus?"

"Gus was still in school when his father started working at Beachside."

"I remember his family moving to Manly during our last year at high school."

She twisted the end of her ponytail around her finger.

"I was only thirteen and he was one of my youth group leaders for a number of years."

"Okay."

"He was popular—had lots of girlfriends."

"Yeah, Gus wasn't shy when it came to girls."

She circled back around the sofa toward him, meeting his gaze. "Well, when I was nineteen he asked me out."

Zach's frown deepened. "On a date."

She nodded. "He wasn't as involved with the church at that stage but he still called himself a Christian."

He shook his head. "I know where this story is going and I'm sorry. You deserved better."

"As you've guessed, the date didn't end well. He behaved badly, I slapped his face and I didn't see him again until today."

He muttered under his breath. "I'm glad you put him in his place."

"I don't think he appreciated it and I can tell he still remembers that night." She lowered her lashes, hiding the emotional pain lingering in her eyes. "It was the final straw for me. I was fed up with church people behaving badly and I stopped going to church altogether."

Zach rubbed his hand over his jaw. "That was around the time Gus turned his back on the church and his faith."

"Possibly. The thing is, I'd trusted him. I went out on that date against my better judgment." She stared at the floor, her voice shaky. "It wasn't the first time I'd had a date with a so-called Christian guy turn sour because of my moral beliefs."

He shook his head, feeling her pain. "Unfortunately I suspect your story is too common."

"I couldn't stand the hypocrisy. People pretending to be pious in public and doing whatever they pleased in secret behind closed doors." She looked up at him, her gaze defiant. "To be honest, it made me feel sick and angry. I'm far from perfect but at least I tried to do the right thing. I didn't pretend to be something I wasn't."

Zach stood in front of her, placing his hands on her shoulders. He pulled her closer, wanting to bring her comfort. "I know there's nothing I can say that will change the past. I just wish I could do something to make it better."

She tucked her head under his chin, her eyes closed. "Seeing Gus today helped me realize that I need to return to Beachside and not let the past dictate my future."

"That's a big decision."

She stepped back, holding his hands. "It's time. Are you planning to go to church tomorrow?"

"Yes, to the evening service."

"Perfect. I won't tell Julia because she'll make a big deal out of it."

He nodded and laced his fingers through hers. God had answered his prayers, despite Gus being an unsavory part of her past. He hoped and prayed that Billie would have a positive experience at Beachside Community Church tomorrow night.

The following evening Billie sat toward the back of the bustling church with Zach, wishing she was anonymous and could hide in a corner. It seemed like Zach knew everyone in the building, and her arrival in his company had sparked a flurry of curious looks and whispered conversations.

She and Zach stood for the opening song. Julia and Sean were up front with the worship band. It was years since she'd last heard her sister sing in this building, and happy memories flooded back.

The words were familiar from Riverwood church and she joined the congregation in singing along. It felt right to be back in this building, standing beside Zach who had been instrumental in her search to explore her faith in more detail. Their conversations had led her back into a closer relationship with God.

The song ended and Billie settled back in her seat, her shoulders inches away from Zach's arm. She inhaled his expensive cologne, glad to be reunited with him this weekend.

They'd shared a pizza for dinner at her new apartment last night while they unpacked and rearranged furniture. Today they'd met up at Manly Beach midafternoon, walking along the sand from Manly to Queenscliff and back again. Afterward they'd indulged in a triple chocolate waffle cone from an ice cream parlor on The Corso.

Before long, Zach's pastor friend Simon moved to the front of the stage. He recapped the past few weeks' talks from the book of Esther.

Billie leaned forward in her seat, fascinated by Simon's words. He talked about how Esther had kept her Jewish nationality a secret when she entered the palace of King Xerxes.

Her stomach tightened, the secret of her heritage tearing at her heart. Had she known what Wayne was like as a person from the start, she would have followed protocol and approached him through official channels with the truth. Her prejudices against church people had driven her fear of rejection and betrayal.

She closed her eyes, swallowing hard. It was too late now to have regrets. She'd made a mistake. Somehow she had to unravel the truth and deal with the consequences.

Esther's story had a happy ending. God had used her position as queen to help her rescue the Israelites from persecution and bring about justice. Could she build a close and meaningful relationship with Wayne after withholding the truth?

What about Zach? She dragged her teeth over her lower lip, her unease growing. How would he react to hearing the truth, knowing she'd kept it hidden? Could he forgive her for not being transparent and fully honest?

Lord, I don't know what to do. How can I tell Zach and Wayne the truth without losing the opportunity to build a relationship with both of them?

The service ended and she gathered her purse and jacket.

Zach smiled. "What did you think?"

"It's a little different from what I remember. I recognized quite a few people and it feels like everyone has noticed us."

"Yeah, it's a bit of a fishbowl but they'll soon get used to seeing us together."

She nodded, liking the thought of spending more time with Zach.

"Have you met Simon?" he asked.

"At Julia and Sean's wedding. Why?"

"He waved and he's heading our way."

She spun around, a smile on her lips.

Simon moved into the row in front of them. "Hey, Zach, Billie. Good to see you both here tonight."

"You too," Zach said. "Great sermon."

"Thanks. Esther's story is an interesting one." Simon switched his attention to her. "Billie, what did you think?"

"What you said was helpful. I've always been intrigued by the fact that God isn't actually mentioned anywhere in the book of Esther but it's so clear that God plays a major role in Esther's life and her story."

Simon nodded. "Her faith was remarkable and tested by the danger she faced in the palace." He nodded to another member of the congregation. "Unfortunately, I need to see a few people now. Billie, I hope we'll chat again next week."

"Yes, I should be here."

"Great, I'll see you then." Simon hurried away.

Zach held her gaze. "I'm glad you want to come back next week. Do you want to hang around for coffee?"

She shook her head. "Now you're pushing your luck. Can we have a quiet coffee somewhere else, and escape before Julia has a chance to interrogate me?"

He laughed. "Let's go now."

Billie followed Zach to the empty side aisle that led to the closest exit. She looked forward to chatting with Zach over coffee and exploring the content of Simon's talk in more detail.

She raced down the steps outside the church and let out a deep breath. "Where do you want to go?"

He smiled, tucking her hand in his. "I know just the place, a café the church crowd rarely visit on Sunday nights."

"Sounds perfect." She fell into step beside him, glad her phone was switched to silent. She'd ignore messages from her sister and make the most of spending quality time with Zach without any distractions.

Chapter 10

A week later, Billie sipped her latte in a Sydney café and checked her messages in her phone. The hectic lunch crowd at the Martin Place eatery in the city had thinned, the time approaching two in the afternoon.

Zach had hoped to meet her for lunch at one, but something had come up at work to delay him. Monday was her day off work this week. She'd browsed in the stores in the popular Pitt Street Mall shopping district and met Julia for coffee in the historic Queen Victoria Building at eleven.

Julia had quizzed her about her church attendance and relationship with Zach. Billie hadn't provided her sister with satisfactory answers on either count. But her sister had her own interpretation. She believed Zach had serious intentions, and she thought Billie's new commitment to church a step forward in their relationship.

Her phone beeped. She read the message, her mouth drawn into a big smile. Zach was on his way.

Minutes later Zach strode through the café entrance, his elegant business suit adding to his air of authority.

He met her gaze, his face brightening as he strode to her table. "Hey, I'm so sorry to keep you waiting."

"It's okay. I'm glad you were able to escape."

"Have you ordered?"

She shook her head. "I didn't mind waiting because I had something to eat earlier with Julia."

He signaled a waiter, and they placed their order. Billie chose the Thai beef salad and Zach requested a club sandwich.

He glanced at his watch. "I can only stay for a short time because I have a conference call scheduled soon that I can't shift."

"Sure. I understand your job is busy."

He rubbed his hand over his cropped hair, worry lines prominent between his brows. "I feel bad that you came all the way into the city and I hardly have any time to see you."

"It's not a problem. I made the most of the day and I love the Manly ferry trip. Are you working late tonight?"

"Yep. I have work that's due today and a couple of meetings that will chew up my time."

She frowned. "You look exhausted, and it's only Monday."

"My job is nonstop with a constant to-do list that never gets any shorter."

The waiter returned with their lunch.

Zach took a large bite from his sandwich, looking like he was ravenous.

"Did you have time for breakfast?" she asked.

He nodded. "At home, before I caught the seven-thirty ferry. I haven't had a chance to stop and eat until now."

She sampled her Thai beef salad, the zesty sweet chili dressing pleasing her palate. "This is good."

"I'm glad you like it." He sipped his cappuccino. "How about I make it up to you tomorrow night? We could go somewhere nice for dinner in Manly."

Her heart skipped a beat. "I'd like that, but are you sure you won't get stuck in the office?"

"Tomorrow should be okay, unless something unexpected crops up."

"I'm at the clinic until six."

"Okay, I'll meet you at the clinic, and message you if I'm running late and miss the ferry."

She speared a grape tomato with her fork. "That works for me."

Zach ate the last portion of his sandwich and his phone beeped. He groaned, checking the screen. "I'm sorry, I have to go back to work now. Would you like anything else? I'll settle the bill on my way out."

She shook her head. "I'm fine, thank you. I'm glad I had a chance to see you."

"Me too." He drank the rest of his cappuccino and stood. "I'll message you later."

"Sure, I hope your day goes well."

"Thanks, I'll be in touch."

He strode over to the counter, his tailored suit highlighting his broad shoulders and lean waist. A number of female glances flicked in his direction.

Billie suppressed the urge to join him at the counter, claiming him as her man.

Her man. She'd been back in Sydney for ten days and had discovered his banking career was all consuming. The carefree, relaxed Zach she remembered from Sapphire Bay had reappeared on the weekends. During the week he was all business, focused on achieving his task list.

She drained her latte glass and returned Zach's wave as he left the café. His current job didn't provide him with a lot of time to grow and nurture a relationship. Was this the life she wanted, snatching time with him between meetings and work commitments?

The next day, Billie finished up with her last patient and processed the credit card payment at the clinic's reception desk. Zach was on the Manly ferry and due to arrive at the wharf in fifteen minutes. The other podiatrists had gone home earlier and she'd completed most of the end-of-day tasks.

Her elderly patient left and she cleaned up her exam room before updating her patient notes. Her day had been routine with ingrown toenail procedures, diabetes check-ups, orthotic fittings and sports injuries.

The main door opened and she gasped. Zach walked into the clinic, holding an exquisite boxed arrangement of pink lilies and blue irises.

She stood, her smile wide. "Zach, wow, they're a stunning combination."

"Vibrant and pretty. I found this arrangement and thought of you."

"Thank you. I'm impressed you made it here on time."

"I had a better day at work with no unexpected surprises." He passed over the box, his fingertips grazing hers.

A jolt of awareness shot through her and she held his warm gaze. "That's good. My day was normal, and I'm getting back into the routine of working here again."

"Is it very different from Riverwood?"

"Not really, except here I've known many of my patients for a couple of years and it's nice to chat with the regulars."

She placed the flowers on the desk and shut down the computer. "What are our plans for tonight?"

"It's up to you. What do you feel like eating?"

"I don't know, but I'm hungry." She picked up her purse and jacket, locating her keys in her purse.

"We could visit the new Japanese restaurant opposite the beach. I've heard the sushi is good."

"I won't say no to sushi."

"I thought so. Let's get moving."

She locked up the clinic and walked down the street

with Zach, making their way toward The Corso and Manly Beach.

He held the flowers, a sweet reminder of his thoughtful gesture.

The ocean breeze whipped up and she slipped her jacket on. A vivid sunset of pinks and oranges streaked the fluffy clouds in the sky.

"Are you warm enough?" he asked.

She nodded, pausing at the pedestrian traffic lights. "My car is in the parking garage at work. I can drive you home after dinner."

"Thank you. You know, we could put your flowers in your car now, before dinner."

"Yes, but I'd like to enjoy looking at them over dinner."

He smiled. "I'm glad you like them."

"They're special because they're from you."

His face relaxed, the tension and stress from his busy work schedule seeming to dissipate.

The pedestrian light changed to green and they joined the flow of people walking toward The Corso. Palm trees swayed overhead in the gusty breeze. Aromas from a variety of restaurants filled the air, rousing her appetite.

He laced his fingers through hers and she fell into step beside him. It seemed right to be heading out to dinner with him after work, as if they were a couple. Their relationship was still undefined, although they messaged each other at least once a day and spent as much time together as possible.

Zach slowed his pace as they approached the oceanfront. "We now have a sailing date planned with Julia and Sean."

"Your yacht's back in the water?"

He nodded. "As of this weekend. Julia suggested we

have a late Sunday lunch on the yacht. They have church commitments in the morning."

"Okay. I'm looking forward to seeing your yacht."

"She should be looking great, all polished and spruced up."

"I can't wait." A day out on the water with Zach sounded like a lot of fun. He'd be in his element, at home on the water and in command of his yacht.

On Sunday afternoon Zach lowered the anchor of his yacht in a small cove surrounded by bushland on Sydney Harbour. They'd spent an hour sailing around the harbor. Sean had helped him with the yacht while the sisters chatted and enjoyed the ride.

His gaze rested on Billie, her straw hat protecting her face from the sun. Sunglasses shaded her eyes and she seemed comfortable moving around the deck. The light wind was predicted to pick up speed later in the afternoon.

He sat beside Billie on a bench seat. "Can you help me set up the table for lunch?"

"Sure. Is everything we need in the picnic basket and cooler bags?"

"I think so." Zach pulled out the folding table in the cockpit between the two bench seats. "Julia organized our lunch."

Julia smiled. "It's only sandwiches, nothing exciting. I hope that's okay?"

Sean appeared from inside the cabin. "That works for me." He passed over a large picnic basket and two cooler bags.

The girls organized the table and before long they had consumed a delicious selection of sandwiches.

Billie leaned back in her seat, stretching her bare arms over her head. "Jules, thanks for preparing our lunch."

"You're welcome. I also brought some fruit. Bananas, apples and sliced watermelon."

"Sounds great." Billie selected two crisp Pink Lady apples from the cooler bag, passing one over to Zach.

"Thanks." He bit into the juicy apple, his favorite variety.

Julia's gaze shifted between him and Billie. "How did you know Zach wanted an apple?"

Billie shrugged. "We have lunch together a lot and I know what he likes."

He laughed, savoring the sweet apple flavor. "Your sister is smart and she looks after me."

Sean turned to his wife, eyebrows raised. "So, where's my piece of fruit? You should know what I like, too."

Julia narrowed her eyes, a smile hovering on her lips. "You're too unpredictable, and could want any or all of the options I brought along."

Billie chuckled and continued munching on her apple. "Julia has a point. I never know if I've chosen the right thing to cook you for dinner."

Sean grinned. "I'll eat anything you cook."

"Me too." Zach finished off his apple and tossed the core in the trash bag. "Who wants to row into shore and explore the beach?"

Billie's smile widened. "Me. I haven't been to that little beach in ages."

Julia opened a container of sliced melon. "Is it okay if I stay on the yacht? I feel like having a nap on the warm deck."

Sean held his wife's hand, concern shadowing his face. "Are you feeling okay?"

Julia nodded. "I'm a little tired, that's all. I've had a busy week and sailing often makes me feel sleepy."

"I'll stay here with you," Sean said. "Zach and Billie can explore the beach together."

"Sounds good." Zach stood. "Billie, are you ready?"

"Yep. We'll be back soon."

"Take your time," Julia said. "We're in no rush to go anywhere."

Zach ducked over to the side of his yacht. He hauled the rowboat closer. "I'll board first and help you down."

"Thanks," Billie said.

He climbed down the ladder and stepped into the middle of the six-seater boat.

Billie followed and he held out his hand, helping steady her.

She sat opposite him on the bench seat, regaining her balance, her hand lingering in his grip.

He picked up the oars and rowed toward the secluded beach, missing the warmth from her fingers entwined with his. "It looks like we'll have the beach to ourselves."

"A nice change from the crowded ocean beaches. I long for the open spaces at Sapphire Bay."

"Me too." He reached the shallow water, holding an oar vertical to discern the depth. "I'll jump out and pull the boat in closer to shore. You may get a little bit wet."

"No problem." She trailed her hand through the clear salty water. "The water feels like a nice temperature."

"It's not bad for this time of year." He jumped out of the boat into knee-deep water, his feet sinking into the soft sand. He pulled the boat farther up the beach and held out his hand.

"Thanks." She stepped into the water, the gentle waves skimming the hem of her knee-length shorts.

He secured the boat on the sand. Dense foliage shaded a large section of the shore. "We could walk around the rocks toward the headland."

"Sounds fun." She angled closer to him, her fingertips reaching for his hand.

He walked by her side, welcoming her touch. The swell in the water strengthened as they neared the entrance to the harbor.

They detoured away from the water on dry sand behind large boulders, his yacht disappearing from view as they faced the wide expanse of ocean.

A whisper-light breeze circled around them and she tucked a few loose strands of her lustrous hair behind her ears.

A couple of fins appeared in the choppy ocean water. He paused, shoving his sunglasses on his head and moving toward the water to take a closer look. "Wow, did you see that?"

"See what?" She removed her sunglasses and hat, her head turned to follow his line of vision.

"In the water near South Head."

She gasped. "Dolphins. How many are there?"

"It looks like a pod."

"I thought they only visited the harbor in the winter months."

"It depends. I've seen dolphins from my yacht in the harbor at different times of the year." The dolphins appeared to take turns, leaping into the air and playing together in the water.

"They look like they're having lots of fun. I wish I had my phone to take photos."

He laughed, resting his arm over her shoulders. "It's always the way, no camera when we need it."

"True."

He stood beside her, the dolphins capturing their full attention. He sneaked a glance in her direction, her face animated as she enjoyed their graceful antics in the water.

She looked up at him, her eyes soft. "I wonder if Julia and Sean can see the dolphins from the yacht."

"Maybe." He held her gaze. "It depends on what they're doing and if they're looking in the right direction."

She nodded, turning her back on the water and dolphins to face him.

He stared at her mouth, her moist lips slightly parted. "Can I kiss you?"

Her eyes widened and she dropped her sunglasses and hat on the sand. "Yes."

Chapter 11

Billie sucked in a shallow breath, her attention focused on the man standing in front of her on the isolated harbor beach. She placed her hand on Zach's cheek, her fingertips tracing the light stubble on his jaw.

Zach lowered his head, his eyes molten and intent on her lips. She closed her eyes, his gentle touch on her mouth sending a shiver over her warm skin.

She deepened the kiss. He pulled her closer, one hand firm on her waist and the other entwined in her loose hair.

She ran her hand over his cropped hair, a deluge of feelings crashing over her.

He pulled back and took a deep breath.

Wow. She opened her eyes, wanting to stay in his arms and reluctant to return to the real world.

"Billie." His eyes softened. "You're amazing. I've wanted to kiss you properly for a long time."

Her heart skittered to a faster rhythm and she tried to pull together her scattered thoughts. "I'm happy you did. You sure know how to kiss."

He laughed. "I'm glad you approve."

She nodded, unable to deny her strong feelings for Zach. The secret she carried dampened part of her enthusiasm. Sooner rather than later she needed to put together a plan for revealing the truth to Wayne and Zach. But she didn't want to risk fracturing the precious relationship she'd developed with Zach over the past few months.

He draped his arm over her shoulders, pulling her closer to his side. "We probably should head back to the yacht before your sister sends out a search party looking for us."

"Yes, they can't see us here."

He grinned. "Privacy can be a good thing."

"Absolutely." She dropped down on her knees and picked up her hat and sunglasses. Thankfully the small cove was protected from the harsh sea winds. If Julia knew about the incredible kiss she'd shared with Zach, she'd drill her with questions and premature wedding plans.

Zach helped her to her feet, and they walked hand in hand back around the rocks toward the small rowboat.

She tipped her face up, desperate to ask the one question smoldering in her mind. "Where does this leave us?"

"In a good place." His voice deepened. "I hope you'll consider coming along to the beach volleyball youth group event next weekend."

She pursed her lips. "But I'm not a youth leader?"

"Not a problem. A number of people our age will be there to help out, and it's a good opportunity to get to know a few more Beachside regulars in a casual setting."

Billie nodded, her doubts starting to rise. She squashed them down. If she wanted to be in a relationship with Zach, she had to enter his world and meet his friends. She needed to give churchgoers a chance to regain her trust.

"Are you free next Saturday afternoon at four?" he asked.

"Yes, but will you be finished sailing by then?"

"I'm not racing next weekend. You can come over to the clubhouse with me beforehand, if you're interested. There are a few things I'll need to do on the yacht but it won't take long."

"You're not taking her out sailing?"

"I can, if you're keen?"

"Why not? Sailing is fun."

"Okay, and there's one more thing."

"Oh, you're sounding very serious."

"My mother is dying to meet you and she's busy planning my thirtieth birthday party." He paused. "I hope you can come to my party."

"Of course, I wouldn't miss celebrating your birthday. Where is your party being held?" She tried to keep her voice casual, but her heart had picked up the moment Zach mentioned meeting his parents.

"At my parents' home. My mom wants us to have dinner with the family sometime over the next few weeks, before my birthday."

"I'm sure we can find an evening that works."

"Great. My father and sisters really want to meet you, too."

"You have three younger sisters, right?"

"Yep. They're a big reason why I moved out of home as soon as I could afford my own place."

She giggled. "One sister is enough for me. I can't imagine having three."

"Put it this way, my family home is chaotic, plus they all still live at home."

"And none of them have married?"

He shook his head. "I'm a few years older than the girls and our mother is very protective of them."

"It sounds like it will be an interesting meal."

"Don't say I didn't warn you."

She leaned closer to him, her head resting on his arm as they walked toward the rowboat. She looked forward to meeting Zach's family and learning more about his background. Beach volleyball next weekend should be fun.

* * *

The following Saturday Billie stood at the volleyball net, her feet anchored in the fine sand on Shelly Beach in Manly. Zach was beside her on the court, coaching the teens on their team. They were in the lead, one point away from winning the game. Smoke from the grill wafted in their direction. A few of the older teams manned dinner prep. Her team member served deep into the court and the ball came back over the net in Billie's direction. She leaped into the air, spiking the ball into a gap in the sand between their opponents.

"Yes." She regained her balance, her fist raised. "We did it."

Zach gave her a big high five, a triumphant grin covering his face. "Well done. I'm impressed by your abilities."

She nodded. "Don't forget I grew up playing volleyball with this youth group."

Their team members congratulated each other and their opponents before walking toward the grassy area near the grill.

Zach placed his hands on his hips. "I'm discovering your hidden talents."

"I liked playing sports at school. Volleyball is fun."

She strolled beside him to the larger group and chewed on her lip. Everyone seemed to know that she was with Zach, and the youth group leaders had so far welcomed her involvement in the group's activities. She was starting to wonder if the hypocrisy she'd witnessed was more rare than she'd thought.

He placed his hand on her forearm. "I just remembered I need to get something from my SUV."

"Okay, I'll come with you."

"No, you can stay here and chat. Ginny and Kristin

are heading our way." Zach took off in the direction of his SUV.

Billie narrowed her eyes, glad she was wearing sunglasses. Kristin was a sweetheart but Ginny had been her tormenter in youth group. The queen of the mean girls. She'd tried to stay out of Ginny's way at church, and it looked like she wouldn't be able to avoid her.

Kristin smiled, her face flushed in the late afternoon sunlight. "Billie, you played really well. I wish I still had your level of fitness."

She nodded. "Thanks. I like taking long walks and working out at the gym."

Ginny crossed her arms over her chest. "I don't know how you find the time. My job keeps me so busy that I just can't fit regular workout sessions into my schedule."

"That's a shame." Ginny's family owned a popular Manly restaurant and she worked as a flight attendant. Her lean physique was unchanged from high school and she wore the latest fashion.

"Well." Ginny tipped her nose in the air. "It's good to see you've come back to church. Zach seems to be a good influence on you."

Billie bristled, the tone in Ginny's voice reminiscent of the past. "Actually, I started going back to church before I met Zach."

Kristin giggled. "I think you two make a cute couple. We've been wondering for years when Zach would finally decide to settle down."

Ginny's mouth thinned. "You've done well to catch Zach. Many others have tried and failed. But, you always managed to attract all the boys. And they really liked dating you."

"Ginny!" Kristin said. "That's not a nice thing to imply."

Billie stood taller, her hands balled into fists. "Especially when it's not true."

"You can drop the sweet and innocent act with me," Ginny said. "We all know about your past."

Billie shook her head. "The gossips got it wrong."

"I heard it firsthand," Ginny said. "You remember Angus, of course."

She clenched her jaw. "I remember slapping his face because he deserved it."

Ginny smirked. "That's not how he described your date. I wonder if he told Zach what he told me."

Billie inhaled a sharp breath, struggling to hold back her anger. "It's time to end this conversation."

Kristin frowned. "Ginny, can you drop it? All this stuff happened years ago."

Ginny shook her head. "It had to be said."

"Why?" Billie bit her lower lip. "Gus hasn't told you the truth about what happened. You've always hated me, and you know what? I don't care what you think."

Ginny gasped. "You should care about your reputation."

Billie straightened her back, reaching her full height. "Not when it's based on lies. This is idle gossip. We're grown women and should be past this."

"But your reputation will reflect badly on Zach."

Kristin grabbed Ginny's arm. "Billie, I'm really sorry and I don't agree with Ginny. It's time for us to help serve up dinner. I'll catch up with you later, okay?"

Billie nodded and stared at the patchy grass. Did the mean girls ever grow up?

Ginny and Kristin walked toward the grill, leaving her alone.

Billie blinked away the moisture in her eyes and drew in a calming breath. Ginny's words didn't have the power to hurt her anymore. *Lord, please help me to let it go and not allow Ginny's words and attitude to undermine or upset me.*

Within minutes Zach returned to her side. "Did you have a chance to talk with the girls?"

She nodded. "Kristin is really nice and she wants to chat with me later. Did you find what you needed in your SUV?"

"All sorted. Are you hungry?"

"Yep." She forced her mouth into a smile. "What's on the menu?"

"Probably burgers. Let's join the line and find out."

The next hour passed quickly. Billie stayed as far away from Ginny as possible, determined to not even look in her direction. She kept her smile in place, the friendliness of the other church members taking the sting out of Ginny's comments. She was determined to give church a second chance, though Ginny wasn't making it easy.

The youth group event came to an end and Billie relaxed her posture. She'd survived Ginny's taunts and made a couple of new friends during dinner.

Billie walked with Zach to his SUV. The cool evening sea breeze blew her hair across her face, and she swiped at the flyaway strands.

"What do you want to do now?" Zach asked.

"We could go to the movies? I'll need to go home first and get changed into something warmer."

He opened her door. "Which movie would you like to see?"

She stepped up into the passenger seat. "Isn't it your turn to pick a movie?"

He grinned. "You might regret making that offer."

"I'm sure your choice will be fine. As long as it's not horror."

"You don't like scary movies?"

"Not particularly." Dealing with Ginny today and standing up to her bullying tactics was scary enough.

He walked around the front of his SUV before settling beside her in the driver's seat.

She clicked her seatbelt into place. "How well do you know Ginny?"

"Probably about as well as I know Julia. Why?"

"I was just wondering."

He stuck his key in the ignition and turned to face her. "What happened?"

She kept her smile intact, unwilling to let Ginny's words ruin her night. "She helped me realize that the small stuff doesn't matter. I don't need Ginny, or anyone else, to like me."

"Whoa, what exactly did Ginny say?"

"She mentioned some stuff from the past that wasn't true."

"Seriously? I'm going to talk to her—"

"No, please leave it alone. I handled it and if you say something, she'll think her words got to me."

He rubbed his hand over his jaw. "Okay, but I want to know if she says anything else that's inappropriate. It's not acceptable for her to do this to you."

"Honestly, Zach, it's not a big deal. I had wondered if you were good friends or had dated in the past."

He shook his head, his mouth pulled into a straight line. "I've never really taken much notice of her."

She nodded. His lack of attention had probably inspired Ginny's outburst. "I really don't care what she thinks, and it's liberating. A good thing."

He tucked a few loose strands of her hair behind her ears, his knuckles gentle on her warm cheeks. "Is this what used to happen to you years ago?"

She let out a soft sigh, long forgotten feelings of inadequacy overflowing in her mind. "I'm a big girl now, and I know it's God's opinion that really matters. People like Ginny may have provoked me to walk away from the church years ago. But, I'm not going to let this situation mess with my faith."

He held her hands, his gaze gentle. "I'll do my best to stop people messing with you in any capacity."

"Thank you." She blinked away the tears in her eyes, his words touching her heart. She couldn't bear the thought of losing Zach.

A week later, Zach parked his SUV on the drive and walked with Billie along the path to the front door of his parents' waterfront home. He held her hand, her fingers rigid in his loose grip.

"My parents and sisters are going to love you."

She slowed her pace, her gaze pensive. "I hope so. I'm not sure why I'm feeling so nervous."

"You have nothing to worry about."

"I hope you're right."

He opened the door and led Billie through the foyer into the spacious living room. Large windows and a sliding door provided ocean views to the north from Manly to Queenscliff Beach.

"Zach, you're here on time." His mom hugged him before switching her attention to Billie. "Welcome, Billie. I'm pleased to finally meet you."

Billie smiled. "It's good to meet you, too, Mrs. Montford."

"Please call me Karen. It's pleasant outdoors so I thought we could eat on the deck. The sunset over the water is pretty."

"Sounds lovely," Billie said.

"Mom, can I help you with anything?"

She shook her head, her fair wavy hair pinned back off her face. "Dinner is nearly ready to serve. Lasagna and salad. I hope you'll like it, Billie. Zach's told me you're an excellent cook."

"He flatters me. And yes, lasagna is one of my favorites."

"Very good." His mom's smile broadened. "Zach's father, David, is on a work call in the study. Hopefully he won't be too long and he won't be needed at the hospital."

"Is he on call tonight?" His father was a surgeon who had missed many family dinners due to medical emergencies.

"Yes, but I'm hoping he won't be needed. Your sisters, on the other hand, aren't coming tonight."

He frowned. "What happened? I thought everyone would be here."

"Well, Bek is away for the weekend with friends, a last-minute thing. Kelly messaged me from the Blue Mountains half an hour ago, and she won't be back until much later tonight."

"What about Mel? It's not like her to skip a family dinner."

"You've only just missed her. She's out on a third date, I believe, that was only arranged this afternoon."

He nodded. "What's he like? Do you know much about him?"

Billie giggled. "You sound like the dad."

"I've always looked out for my sisters."

His mom grinned. "He seems all right. Your father put him through his paces tonight, making sure he was worthy of your sister's time and attention."

"Poor Mel. I hope Dad didn't scare him off."

Billie shifted her weight from one foot to the other. "Should I be concerned about meeting your father?"

His mom shook her head. "He's a little overprotective of the girls, and he has met Julia so you've already been vetted."

"Phew, you had me worried for a minute," Billie said.

Zach squeezed her hand. "It's all good. Mom, I'll organize our drinks while we're waiting for Dad."

"Thanks, Zach. There's a jug of iced tea ready to serve."

He located four glasses and the iced tea in the kitchen, and prayed his mother would think before she spoke. She was in a mood, no doubt caused by one of his sisters. Possibly Kelly, who had a tendency to make reckless decisions that upset their mother.

He returned to the living room with a drinks tray, only to discover his mother and Billie were already seated on the deck. He headed outdoors and poured their drinks before sitting beside Billie.

His mom sipped her iced tea. "Perfect. Now Billie, I hear you're a podiatrist. I must remember to look you up the next time I need to see someone."

"Sure. Our clinic has expanded over the last few years."

"Podiatry is a good, practical career. I'm really happy that you've met Zach, and I think you'll be good for him."

"Mom, you're going to scare Billy away because she'll think my family is crazy."

Billie sipped her tea, her gaze lowered.

His mom shook her head. "All families have their quirks. Anyway, I think Billie will be a good influence on you and will help you make smart decisions."

He drew his eyebrows together. "Really? Dare I ask why you think this?"

"Billie, is it true that you're not heavily involved in the church like my son?"

"Um, yes, I guess so." She traced her thumb over the

side of her glass. "I only recently started attending services again. But, I'm not sure how that's relevant—"

"It's totally relevant." His mom rearranged the napkins on the table, her expression neutral.

"Mom, I don't think we should be having this conversation right now."

His mom waved her hand through the air, dismissing his comment. "Of course you don't. Hopefully Billie is sensible enough to convince you that you'd be throwing your life away if you become a pastor."

Chapter 12

Billie gasped, Zach's mother's words circling in her mind. A pastor. Zach wanted to become a pastor. His job in Riverwood now made sense. Why hadn't he shared his aspirations with her?

Zach cleared his throat. "Mom, can we please change the subject and talk about this another time."

"Why?" Karen inspected her immaculate long fingernails. "I'm sure Billie has heard all about your plans for Bible college next year?"

Billie inhaled a deep breath and met Zach's gaze. "What's going on?"

"I haven't said anything because it may not happen. My mother is being presumptuous by bringing up the subject."

"Now Zach, I think it's quite telling that you haven't spoken with Billie. Can I be hopeful and assume you may consider changing your mind?"

He closed his eyes for a few seconds before answering her question in an even tone. "As I told you last year before I went to Riverwood, I don't have any definite plans. Nothing has changed. I'm exploring options but I haven't made any decisions."

Karen stood. "Please excuse me. The lasagna should be ready and I'm going to find out what's keeping David.

I'll be back soon." She headed indoors, closing the sliding door behind her.

Billie's gaze was drawn to the turbulent swell in the ocean. Her heart constricted, knowing he'd chosen to hide his hopes and dreams. Karen had shaken up her world, leading her to question the foundation of her relationship with Zach. Her secret was a big enough problem to navigate without additional complications.

Zach reached for her hand. "I'm sorry. My mother can be difficult but that little performance was over-the-top."

"I understand." His mother had a clear agenda, hoping Billie would take her side against Zach.

"My mom hates the idea of me giving up my banking job. I'm sorry she tried to drag you into the middle."

She turned to him, staring deep into his eyes. "Is it true? Do you really want to be a pastor?"

He nodded. "But, it doesn't mean it will happen. It's a big decision and I'm praying about it."

"So, I take it this means you haven't applied to Bible college for next year."

"Yes, and I haven't said anything to you because I'm not sure what I want to do. Work is going really well and I like my job."

She squeezed his hand. "It's okay. I can understand why you haven't said anything." If only she'd been honest with him from the start, and pushed aside her fears to reveal her secret.

He looked her straight in the eye, his expression serious. "Are you comfortable with the idea that I might throw in my banking career and go to Bible college?"

She sipped her iced tea. "Honestly, I don't know. Unlike my sister, I've never had aspirations to become a pastor's wife."

His eyebrows shot up and he remained silent.

She bit her lip. Why did she have to bring up the subject of marriage? They'd tiptoed around the topic by letting their friendship evolve into a more serious relationship. She wasn't ready to risk rejection by revealing the truth in her heart.

The sliding door opened and Karen reappeared with a tray of lasagna, accompanied by Zach's father, who juggled a salad bowl and garlic bread.

Billie fidgeted with her napkin and drew in a soothing breath. Zach had schooled his features into a neutral expression, his attention focused on his meal.

David smiled and shook her hand. "Hi, Billie. I'm sorry I was delayed by the call. It's good to finally meet you."

She smiled. "You too."

Karen served up the lasagna on white porcelain plates. "I enjoyed chatting with Billie earlier."

David unfolded a linen napkin. "Billie, I hear you like sailing."

"Yes, it's fun."

"Dad, we're planning to go out tomorrow, if the weather is fine."

David nodded. "A good idea."

Karen refilled their glasses of iced tea. "Zach, have you thought about what you'll do with your yacht?"

Zach swallowed a mouthful of lasagna. "What do you mean?"

"Looking into the future." Karen added salad to her plate. "If you leave your banking career, how will you afford the expense of keeping your yacht in the years to come?"

"Karen!" David sent his wife a stern look. "Let it go. Our son is old enough to make his own decisions."

"But David, I really think he'd be making a mistake—"

"No, you just can't let go of your prejudices from the past." David shook his head. "That's not fair to Zach."

Billie focused her attention on her plate, the tension in the air palpable. She picked at the delicious lasagna, her appetite waning. What had happened to Karen in the past?

"Mom, what's going on?"

Karen blew out a stream of air. "Okay, I admit that I had a few less than pleasant experiences with a church years ago, before I met your father."

Zach narrowed his eyes. "You've never said anything about this before. Why?"

Karen closed her eyes for a brief moment. "It was a long time ago and I've tried to forget. I believe in God and all, but I just can't stomach the thought of belonging to a church after what happened."

David held his wife's hand, his gaze tender. "We can talk about this another time."

"Mom, I had no idea. You've never said anything until now."

Karen covered her mouth with her hand, her face stricken. "It's too painful. Billie, I'm sorry to unload all this now while you're here. Zach's right, you'll think we're crazy."

She shook her head. "No, I think you're honest and real. I grew up in the church and left five years ago because I was burned."

Karen patted her hand. "Oh honey, I'm sorry bad stuff happened to you, too."

"I'm working through my issues. It's been a slow process but I'm healing. My faith took a battering but I have hope."

Karen sighed. "I've never discouraged my children from attending church. We usually go at Christmas and Easter. But Zach, it's one thing to attend church, and a totally different thing to work for a church and center your life around a church congregation."

He shook his head. "Mom, I wish you'd said something earlier. I had no idea this was a sensitive and personal issue for you."

Billie nibbled on her salad, her heart breaking over the obvious pain in Karen's voice. She empathized with her situation, and her struggle to come to terms with Zach's potential future plans.

Karen sat taller in her seat, her chin tipped up. "Your father is right. It's your life and your choice. My personal grievances aren't your problem. Did you know both Mel and Bek are thinking about switching churches and moving to Beachside?"

"Really?" Zach sipped his drink. "Do you know why?"

"They like what they've heard about the social scene at Beachside, and their friends are thinking about making the move."

David shook his head. "Do they realize churches are not dating services?"

Karen shrugged. "Who knows what our girls think? Anyway, Billie, I'm glad you're able to attend Zach's thirtieth birthday."

Billie smiled, relieved they'd changed the subject. "Yes, I'm looking forward to it."

Zach placed his cutlery on his empty plate. "This is Mom's big project."

Karen's smile lit up her face. "I love throwing parties. Billie, I was wondering if your parents would like to come, too."

"That's really sweet of you to think of them, but unfortunately they won't be back from Europe in time."

"Not a problem. We'll have to invite them over for dinner when they return."

"I'm sure they'd appreciate the invitation." Billie met Zach's gaze, his encouraging smile warming her heart. His parents had accepted her into their family and anticipated that she had a future with their son.

Her throat constricted, her secret creating a painful wedge. She'd deleted half a dozen draft emails to Wayne, the right words not coming to mind. She was still scared. Petrified of rejection, despite the evidence suggesting it was an unlikely outcome.

Lord, please give me the courage to reveal the truth to both Wayne and Zach.

A few days later Zach sat opposite Billie at his dining room table, sharing an early dinner before his church group descended for their midweek meeting in his apartment. He'd escaped work at a reasonable time, for a change, and Billie had given him a lift home from Manly Wharf.

He held her warm gaze, thankful that she was an important part of his life. "I appreciate you providing dinner."

She smiled, dabbing the corner of her mouth with her napkin. "You're welcome. It's not hard to reheat beef stew from my freezer."

"It's delicious." He scraped up the last bits of broth. "Sean and Julia are coming over early because Sean's going to help me resolve an IT issue. They'll be here any minute."

"No problem. I can clean up the mess I've made in your kitchen. Do you need to do any food prep for tonight?"

He shook his head. "I have cookies in the container beside the coffee machine and it's someone else's turn to bring snacks." He rose and helped Billie clear the table. "I'm glad you've decided to meet the group."

She nodded. "I was a teen the last time I attended a small church group."

"I'm praying tonight will be a positive experience for you." He'd only managed to learn the skeleton details from her conversation with Ginny at Shelly Beach. He was disappointed by Ginny's blatant attempt to undermine Billie.

"Thanks. I should be fine. I've brought my leather bound Bible that I found in a box when I unpacked my apartment. Also, your mom called me today to organize a coffee date."

He grinned. "I told you she'd love you."

"I really appreciate the warm welcome into your family. And I'm looking forward to meeting your sisters at your birthday party."

"Yes, they'd better not skip out on my party or my mom will be on their case, big-time." He'd spoken with his mother yesterday, and she'd shared a little more about her past church experiences. He was disgusted to learn that a pastor had been one of the people who had hurt his mom, primarily through church teachings that weren't consistent with the Bible.

Billie stood and stacked their dinner plates. "Would you like a coffee now?"

He shook his head. "I can wait."

The doorbell buzzed and he glanced at his watch. "That will be Sean and Julia. I'll go let them in."

"Please tell Julia I'll be in the kitchen."

"Okay." He strode to his front door, happy that Sean had offered to help him fix a networking problem with his computer.

His phone beeped, a message from Mel. He should try to introduce Billie to his sisters before his birthday. His mom had embraced Billie into the family as if she was her own daughter, and he prayed he could soon make that a reality.

He loved Billie, and he couldn't imagine her not being

in his life. She wasn't thrilled by his ambitions to work as a pastor, but that was something they could negotiate and work through over time.

Billie arranged a dozen side plates and coffee mugs on Zach's kitchen counter. She'd cleaned up the kitchen and stored the leftover beef stew in the fridge.

Over the weekend Gus had taught her how to use Zach's fancy coffee machine. Gus had settled down, acknowledging that she was a part of Zach's life. She'd let his inappropriate comments from their first meeting in Zach's apartment slide, despite learning that he may have lied to Ginny years ago.

It was possible Ginny had lied about Gus, too. She'd avoided Ginny at church, refusing to be drawn into any public disputes. Ginny's immaturity was not her problem, and she could now see how Ginny had manipulated her when they were younger.

It wasn't worth the angst of dredging up the past and rehashing issues that weren't important. Some people were going to do the wrong thing and hurt others, irrespective of their faith, or whether or not they attended church.

Gus had turned his back on the church, and had admitted to her that he struggled with his faith. His strict and conservative pastor father didn't approve of his lifestyle choices, which had created problems in Gus's relationship with both of his parents. The unrealistic expectation of being the perfect pastor's kid had fueled his teenage rebellion.

Julia appeared in the kitchen, an expectant smile on her face. "Hey, Billie. It's great to see you here tonight."

"You too." She hugged her sister. "It's been a while since we've had a chance to chat."

"I know. So, what's happening with you and Zach? You

do realize you're the main topic of conversation and speculation at Beachside."

She rolled her eyes. "People have too much time on their hands. Haven't they got more interesting things to talk about?"

"Obviously not. I assume you haven't heard what's being said?"

"Nope, and I really don't care. I have low expectations regarding people's behavior and I'm just not interested in hearing the gossip."

"Well, this time you'll probably appreciate the heads-up."

"Why? What are they saying?"

Julia twisted her hands together. "The big rumor doing the rounds is that Zach's going to propose to you during his birthday party."

Her jaw fell slack. "Seriously? People are talking about us getting married?"

"You shouldn't be too surprised. Everyone knows you two are inseparable and head over heels. It's only a matter of time until Zach pops the question."

Billie crossed her arms over her torso and leaned back against the kitchen counter. "You know that won't happen while our parents are overseas."

"Of course. Sean and I have said nothing, and we refuse to be drawn into the speculation."

"Over the weekend I learned that Zach has ambitions to become a pastor."

Julia's eyes widened. "Oh, you didn't know that? How do you feel about his plans?"

She pressed her lips together. "I don't know if I want to become a pastor's wife."

"You make it sound like a life sentence."

"At the moment it's only an idea that he's exploring."

"Do you think he might change his mind?"

She shrugged. "It's complicated, on a number of levels. We have a few big issues to work through before we can make a decision about our future."

"I'll be praying. I highly recommend married life and I think Zach's the one for you. Don't let him go unless you have a really good reason to walk away."

"I've been taking baby steps to reconnect with the church community. It hasn't all been smooth sailing, but I think this time I have realistic expectations. I expect people to behave badly and I'm not going to let that affect my faith."

"Wow." Her sister shook her head. "Six months ago I'd never have anticipated you speaking these words."

"I've also made my peace with Gus."

"Who's Gus?"

"Angus. He's staying here with Zach."

"Oh, yeah. He disappears when our group visits and I haven't seen him at Beachside in years. But, I don't remember you having anything much to do with him."

"You never heard any gossip?"

Julia shook her head. "Not a word."

"That's good." It looked like Ginny had made up stories about Gus, too.

"Is there something I should know?"

"No, I'm leaving the past in the past."

"It's a much better idea to focus on the present and the future. An exciting future, by the sounds of it."

"We'll see. Don't start planning a wedding yet."

Julia grinned. "I'm going to see if the boys need anything. Be back soon."

Billie wandered into the living room and stared out at the glittering evening view of the harbor. Lights twinkled in the distance and a ferry glided into Manly Wharf.

She'd set a deadline of writing to Wayne after Zach's birthday. She didn't want to do anything now that could spoil Zach's birthday celebrations, especially if everyone was watching her and Zach. His mother had spent hours on the preparations to make it a special and joyous occasion.

She had a full weekend off work scheduled two weeks after Zach's birthday party. A good opportunity to plan a trip to Riverwood, hopefully with Zach. She could tell Zach first, and make him promise to not say anything to Wayne until she could see her birth father in person.

She dreaded Zach's reaction to her secret, and prayed he would understand why she'd done it this way. Each day she despised herself for not having the courage to speak up earlier. Was there a way to turn this situation around without jeopardizing her future relationships with Zach and Wayne?

Chapter 13

Zach chatted with his mom in the foyer next to the entrance to his parents' living room. A refreshing evening breeze cooled the crowded room through the open deck doors. Contemporary music played in the background and the guests attending his thirtieth birthday party gathered indoors and out on the deck overlooking the ocean.

Billie stood across the room in his direct line of vision. She wore a stunning knee-length red dress and high heels, her hair flowing loose over her shoulders. He'd introduced Billie to his sisters last week, and for the past half hour they'd monopolized all of her time.

His mom patted his forearm. "Zach, have you listened to a word I've said?"

"Huh." He switched his attention back to his mom and adjusted the collar of his long-sleeved shirt. "I'm sorry, you said something about the caterers."

She placed her hand on his cheek. "Can you keep your eyes off Billie long enough to listen to me?"

He grinned. "Okay, you now have my full attention."

"The caterers will be serving the spit roast at eight from the dining room. We'll bring out your birthday cake around nine, followed by dessert. It looks like most of our guests have arrived and all of our family is here."

"Sounds great. Thanks again for all the work you're putting into my party."

"You're welcome. Do you have any friends who are coming later? Will I need to set aside food for them?"

He shook his head. "I think nearly everyone is here. Ryan and Cassie's flight from Queensland was delayed, but they should be here soon."

"I only recently discovered that Julia is married to Ryan's brother. Was that the wedding you missed before you went to Riverwood?"

He nodded. "Speaking of Riverwood, I haven't seen Wayne yet, either. He's traveling up from Riverwood today."

"You're talking about the pastor?"

"Yes, and he's a decent guy. I think you'll like him and I hope you'll take time to talk with him."

"Of course." She tipped her head to the side. "I wonder why he's coming alone. We invited the whole family and it seems odd to travel all this way by himself."

"His boys may have other commitments this weekend."

"True. Anyway, I'll watch the door for the latecomers while you try to wrestle Billie away from your sisters."

He chuckled. "Thanks, Mom. I'm glad you all like Billie."

His mom smiled. "You've chosen well. I'm anxious for grandchildren so you'd better not take too long to put a ring on her finger."

"All in good time. You can do me a favor and dispel the rumors floating around that I'm going to propose to Billie tonight."

"Okay. Her parents will be back from Europe soon and we can plan your engagement party together."

"Don't worry, I'll tell you and Dad first when I decide to take that step."

His mom hugged him close. "I'm so proud of you. I

still can't believe my baby boy is turning thirty tomorrow. Where did the years go?"

He dropped a kiss on his mom's cheek. "Catch you later."

Zach made his way across the living room, stopping a number of times to talk with his friends and family. It seemed like nearly all of the eighty invited guests had turned up. He grabbed a Coke from a waiter circulating with a tray of drinks and sidled up beside Billie.

Billie's eyes sparkled. "Bek has been telling me a few stories about you."

He sipped his Coke. "She has a big mouth."

Bek folded her arms over her chest. "No I don't. It's fun to tell Billie all about the real you."

"I'm sure you've bored her for long enough."

Mel stifled a giggle. "Give Bek a break."

He draped his arm around Billie's shoulders. "You'll soon learn my sisters like to gang up against me. They always stick together."

Kelly flicked a few locks of her fair hair off her face. "That's because Zach is the golden boy and Mom's favorite who can do no wrong."

"Actually, Mom isn't particularly happy with me at the moment. We often don't agree on important issues."

Mel nodded. "She ranted for ages about you going to Bible college. Are you still planning to do that?"

Billie's body stiffened, her gaze directed at the floor.

He drew in a deep breath. "Nothing is definite. She'll calm down, eventually."

Kelly's eyes lit up. "I have to go see someone."

Bek grabbed Kelly's arm. "I'm coming with you." She rushed away with her sister, whispering in Kelly's ear.

Mel smiled. "I'm glad you haven't let Mom stop you from doing what you believe is important."

"I knew you'd understand, and I feel bad that you were on the receiving end of her rant."

"It's okay. Mom explained why she was ranting, which totally shocked me. Had she told you before what had happened years ago?"

He shook his head. "It was news to me, too."

"Okay," his sister said. "I'll leave you two to mingle and I'll make sure Mom isn't stressing over the party. I think Dad has abandoned her to hang out with our uncles."

"Thanks, Mel. I'll see you later."

His sister disappeared into the crowd and he turned to Billie. "Are you enjoying the party?"

"Yep. Your sisters are quite entertaining."

"That's one way of describing them."

Julia waved, walking over to Billie's side. "I was heading over here and was sidetracked talking to the Beachside crowd."

Sean joined his wife. "Great party, Zach."

"Thanks, it seems to be going well."

Julia's phone beeped and she checked the screen. "Cassie and Ryan are at the front door."

Zach gave his empty glass to a passing waiter, his gaze sweeping the entrance to the room. "My mom is chatting with them now."

Cassie and Ryan weaved their way through the crowd, heading in their direction.

Julia let out a squeal and embraced Cassie in an enthusiastic hug. "I'm so glad you both could make it."

"Me too." Cassie gave Zach a brief hug. "Happy Birthday."

"Thanks." He shook Ryan's hand. "It's good to see you guys again. It has been a while."

Ryan nodded. "I've done a number of short trips to

Sydney for work this year, with no time to see anyone or do anything."

"Yes," Cassie said. "The resort's going really well and keeping me busy. You'll have to fly up to Queensland sometime and visit."

"A great idea for when I can manage to take another break from work."

Billie sipped her drink. "Who can say no to a Queensland holiday?"

Cassie clapped her hands together. "I'm so excited I can finally share some news. Laura and Greg are expecting a baby."

Julia bounced up and down. "Yay, I'm so happy for your sister. Wonderful news for your family."

"I can't wait to become an aunt. She's only twelve weeks along, so it's still a while off."

Billie's smile lit up her eyes. "Congratulations. Does this mean you'll have an excuse to visit Sydney more often?"

"I hope so," Ryan said. "I miss being out on the harbor. Zach, I'd ask if I could borrow your yacht tomorrow, or tag along with you, if Laura hadn't already planned out our entire day."

He raised an eyebrow. "Laura won't go sailing?"

Cassie wrinkled her nose. "Morning sickness. Even car travel is making her feel really sick."

"Poor Laura," Billie said. "I hope she starts feeling better soon."

"Me too." Cassie turned to Julia. "I'll message you tomorrow when I know what Laura has planned. I want to see you again before I fly home on Monday morning. Ryan is staying on until Wednesday."

Julia smiled. "That works for me."

Zach glanced at the familiar faces surrounding him,

appreciating the festive atmosphere. Wayne stood on the far side of the room with his mother. "Please excuse us. Billie and I will be back soon."

"No problem," Julia said.

Billie held his hand, her brows furrowed. "Where are we going?"

"Wayne is here."

"Oh." She lowered her lashes and walked with him toward the front of the house. "You didn't mention he was coming tonight."

"He wasn't certain he could make it and he's here by himself."

"Really? That's interesting."

"My mom thought so too. I'm glad he could make it."

Zach smiled, meeting Wayne's warm gaze. "Hey, it's good to see you."

Wayne nodded. "Happy Birthday. Your parents have a beautiful home."

His mom grinned. "Why, thank you. It's a pleasure to meet you, and I hope you enjoy the party. I need to check up on the caterers."

"Thanks, Mom."

His mom rushed away and Billie continued to stare at the floor.

Wayne's gaze rested on Billie. "I'm glad I could be here, and Billie, it's great to see you again, too."

She looked up, her gaze uncertain. "Yes, did you have a good trip? It's a long drive from Riverwood."

"It was okay. I have accommodation booked in Manly tonight and I'll drive home tomorrow."

"Glad you could make it," Zach said. "How is your family doing?"

"The boys are keeping us busy, as usual."

Billie's face paled. "Um, please excuse me. I think I need a drink of water or something."

Zach frowned. "Are you okay?"

"I will be, soon. I'll be back in a few minutes." She spun on her heel and disappeared into the crowd.

Wayne shoved his hands on his hips. "I'm happy to see you and Billie are together."

Zach nodded. "We're taking things slow. My family adores her."

"I'm not surprised. Your mother was telling me she loves throwing parties. Is Billie's birthday coming up soon, or are your sisters' next?"

"Billie's birthday isn't until September."

"What date? Josh has a September birthday."

"September third, a long time away."

Wayne widened his eyes. "That is a long way off. Although, this year seems to be disappearing fast."

"Yep. I still have time to plan something extra special." He hoped to be planning a wedding with Billie by September, if everything fell into place.

Billie stood by herself near the kitchen and drank half a glass of water, her pulse racing. Delaying telling the truth had been easy with Wayne far away. What was she going to do now? She had to return to Zach's side before he became suspicious.

She left her glass with a hovering waiter and barreled back into the crowd. She walked into someone and glanced up, her stomach sinking.

"Hey." Gus grasped her shoulders for a moment, his speculative gaze taking in her flustered appearance. "What has got you all worked up?"

"Nothing." He was too astute for her liking.

"Where's Zach?"

"I'm on my way back to see him."

"You enjoying the party?"

She nodded. "And you?"

"Yep. I recognize a few people from Beachside, but I don't think they're thrilled to see me."

"Don't let them bother you. I think Zach's friends from work and the yacht club are out on the deck."

"I'll be heading back outside soon." He paused. "I admire you for going back."

"Why?"

"I remember how mean some of those girls were to you. It takes courage to go back and face them again."

She curved her mouth into a genuine smile. "I sometimes don't feel very brave."

"Keep your chin up and don't let their narrow-minded ways get to you."

"Great advice. Look, I'd better go and find Zach."

"Sure. Catch you later." Gus stepped past her, heading for the deck.

She let out a sigh, relieved that he hadn't tried to question her further. Zach caught her eye across the room and she maneuvered her way around the guests between them. He was deep in conversation with Wayne. How could she manage to climb out of this tricky situation unscathed?

She moved to Zach's side and pasted a smile on her lips.

Zach placed his hand on her waist. "Are you feeling better?"

She nodded. "A glass of water helped."

Wayne took a sip from his drink. "It's a warm night for this time of year."

"I'm not complaining," Zach said. "We needed the overflow space on the deck."

Wayne smiled. "I can't get over the view. It must look sensational during the day."

"The harbor view from Zach's apartment is amazing, too," she said.

"Zach tells me you're now a regular at Beachside."

"I guess I am. It's my childhood church and in many ways it's the same as I remember."

"I'm glad you're both happy there. Do you miss the beach house at Sapphire Bay?"

"Sometimes," she said. "The serenity and slower pace was a nice change. Sydney is a lot more crowded."

Wayne nodded. "The traffic today was insane. I don't think I could live here again."

"You're from Sydney?" Zach asked.

"Yes, I grew up in the inner suburbs, attended university and Bible college here."

Zach shifted his full attention to Wayne. "Do you still have family in Sydney?"

Billie drew in a sharp breath.

"Yes," Wayne said. "But they're mostly scattered around the outer suburbs. What about you, Billie? Where's your family from?"

"Mainly Sydney."

"That's interesting." Wayne glanced at his watch. "Zach, I promised your mother I'd meet your father and family before dinner is served."

Zach nodded. "It was really good of you to drive all this way."

"Not a problem. Are you both free tomorrow morning?"

Zach turned to her. "Have you made any plans?"

She shook her head, her stomach twisted in a hard knot. "Nothing that can't be changed."

"How about we meet for brunch in Manly? I'm staying at a motel on the oceanfront that's in walking distance to The Corso."

"Great idea," Zach said. "We can all sleep in tomorrow. What do you think, Billie?"

She met Wayne's gaze, her heart rate picking up speed. "Sure. I can make that work."

"How about we meet at ten? Zach, you can message me directions to the café you prefer."

"I'll contact you around nine. Billie and I can work out the details later tonight."

"Okay, I'm looking forward to it." Wayne walked away, swallowed up by the sea of people.

Zach held her close by his side and circulated the room, chatting with his guests. She tried to pay attention but her mind wandered in the direction of her birth father. She watched him from afar, engaging in conversation with Zach's parents and older relations.

She chewed the inside of her cheek, the hearty aroma from the spit roast adding to her nausea. Wayne seemed suspicious of her, but how much could he know? He may not have guessed the truth, but his keen interest in her was undeniable.

Tomorrow, the day of Zach's actual birthday, could be the day her secret blew everything apart. The day she had longed for and dreaded in equal portions. She couldn't keep lying to the two of them. With Wayne right in front of her, the truth was bound to come out.

She gazed up at the handsome man by her side, a man she had grown to love and couldn't imagine life without. She loved Zach with an intensity that had initially scared her and thrilled her. He was her best friend and she trusted him.

Would Zach understand why she had kept this secret close to her heart, a secret she hadn't been prepared to share with anyone?

Billie glanced across the room, her gaze colliding with

Wayne's. He gave her an encouraging smile and she reined in her overactive imagination. All she could do now was pray and trust that God would guide her through the emotional firestorm she had created. She had no one to blame but herself if her relationship with Zach fell apart tomorrow.

Chapter 14

The next morning Billie walked with Zach along the sunny Manly ocean promenade overlooking the sand. A whisper of a breeze tickled her skin and puffy white clouds floated overhead in the sky. Her purse swung on her shoulder, bumping into her waist at regular intervals.

She inhaled the fresh sea air, matching her stride with Zach's. "Would you like your birthday present now, or when we reach Queenscliff?"

He smiled. "You brought it with you?"

She nodded. "Do we have time to stop?" In less than an hour they were due to meet Wayne for brunch.

He pointed to an empty wooden bench seat. "We can sit over there in the shade."

She perched beside him under the towering Norfolk pine and placed her sunglasses on top of her head. "I hope you'll like my gift."

He grinned. "I'm sure I will."

She unzipped her leather purse and retrieved his birthday card. They'd walked together to the beach, joining the many local residents who had ventured out early for a Sunday morning stroll.

"Here it is." She gave him a pale blue envelope. "Happy Birthday."

"Thank you." He leaned toward her, his lips lingering on hers.

She caressed his cheek, her heart melting as his soft lips inspired her to respond to his gentle kiss.

He broke the kiss and stared into her eyes. "I'm happy I can spend my birthday with you."

Her stomach contracted, the angst that had given her a restless night of broken sleep resurfacing. "I'll do my best to make your day perfect."

He opened the envelope, his dimple prominent in his cheek as he examined the gift certificate inside the birthday card. "Wow, this is amazing. You remembered that I wanted to do the bridge climb at dawn."

She nodded. "You'll notice it's for two people."

He dropped a kiss on her lips. "I can't wait to climb the Sydney Harbour Bridge with you by my side."

"Me either."

He leaned back on the bench seat facing the ocean, entwining his fingers through hers. "Have you booked a date for the climb?"

She shook her head. "I wasn't sure about your schedule."

Her anxiety over their brunch date with Wayne had escalated overnight. Did Wayne know the truth? Was it possible that he could have guessed that she was his daughter? Did he know that she was adopted?

Dozens of questions and doubts pressed on her mind. It was logical that he'd want to see Zach today and include her in the invitation. She could be worrying for no reason, but her guilt over withholding this information from Zach remained.

He squeezed her hand. "We should get moving. I've booked a table but I'd prefer to arrive at the café before Wayne."

She stood. "We should make it back in plenty of time."

A group of seagulls hovered nearby and a young family walked past, a baby girl sleeping in the stroller.

Billie's breath caught in her throat, a strong desire to start her own family with Zach filling her heart.

The signage for the popular eatery came into view, and they crossed the busy road to join the crowd already patronizing the café.

She walked up the stairs with Zach to the second level and glanced around the café, unable to see Wayne. They were a few minutes early.

Zach spoke with a waiter, who led them to an outdoor table set for three with a gorgeous view of the sparkling ocean.

She sat beside Zach, an empty seat opposite her and the awning shading their table. She swallowed hard and fidgeted with her sunglasses on the table. She should be enjoying Zach's birthday, celebrating his special day instead of dreading if he'd learn her secret.

"Wayne has just arrived," Zach said.

She nodded, pulling her mouth into a smile. "Are you hungry? I ate a bowl of muesli with yogurt earlier."

He laughed. "Why doesn't that surprise me? I did have a slice of Vegemite toast before I stopped by your apartment."

She glanced at the colorful laminated menu before passing it to Zach. "We needed our energy for the walk."

"True. I think I'll order a hot breakfast."

Wayne appeared beside Zach and shook his hand. "Happy Birthday."

"Thank you. It's great we can catch up this morning."

Wayne took his seat and perused the menu. "I only learned, just before I was leaving your party last night, that today is your actual birthday. I hope I didn't mess with your plans."

He shook his head. "We'll probably go sailing later, if the wind picks up. Unless Billie has a surprise planned that I don't know about?"

She maintained her smile, her nervousness easing. "You'll just have to wait and see."

An efficient waiter arrived at their table and scribbled down their order. She requested an omelet with her cappuccino while the men chose big English-style breakfasts of sausages, bacon and eggs.

Zach opened the blue envelope and passed the gift certificate to Wayne. "This was Billie's birthday surprise for me this morning."

Wayne let out a low whistle. "Very impressive. I've always wanted to do the bridge climb. They started the tours in the late nineties, and by then I'd moved away from Sydney."

"Where were you living?" Zach asked.

"Around Wollongong and the Shoalhaven region, before we moved farther south to Riverwood."

Billie nodded. "The south coast is very pretty."

Wayne handed the gift certificate back to Zach. "When are you planning to visit us again? Billie, the senior ladies at church have asked me to check up on you."

She relaxed her shoulders and curved her mouth into a sincere smile. "Really? They're very sweet."

"Wayne, we'll have to choose a weekend when Billie isn't working."

"In a couple of weeks I have a whole weekend off. We could stay at that lovely bed and breakfast in Sapphire Bay across the road from the beach."

Wayne met her gaze. "You're more than welcome to stay with us in Riverwood. We have two guest rooms and plenty of space."

"I wouldn't want to impose," she said.

"Not at all. My boys miss seeing Zach and we're used to company."

"We can work out the details later," Zach said.

The waiter returned with three cappuccinos.

Wayne sipped his coffee. "So Zach, how's work going?"

"Not bad. It's busy, and I miss the freedom I had at Riverwood to set my own schedule."

They chatted about work and before long their food was served. Her anxiety decreased and she enjoyed talking with Wayne and Zach while she ate.

She formulated a new plan in her mind. She could tell Zach the truth on Friday night and, assuming he accepted her revelation and their relationship survived, she'd plan a trip with Zach to Riverwood to see Wayne the following weekend. Accommodation in Sapphire Bay was essential to avoid an awkward family situation with Wayne's wife and children.

Zach cleared his plate of food and sipped the dregs of his cappuccino. Wayne finished his breakfast and dabbed his mouth with his crisp white linen napkin. "Billie, I have a question for you. What was the main reason for your stay in Sapphire Bay?"

She sucked in a deep breath, his pointed question catching her off guard. "What do you mean?" Her heart pounded and she fumbled for something to say that wasn't an outright lie. Did he know?

Wayne sat taller in his chair. "Billie, we can skirt around this or get to the point. Perhaps you'd prefer to talk to me privately?"

Zach's eyebrows shot up. "Wayne, what's going on? Do you think Billie had an ulterior motive?"

She dug her teeth into her lip, determined to hold her tears at bay. "Zach, it's okay." She turned to Wayne, looking him straight in the eye. "You've guessed the truth, haven't you?"

Wayne's eyes softened. "I had a hunch and Zach confirmed it when he told me the date of your birthday."

She closed her eyes for a few seconds, her mind whirling in a dozen directions. "Are you mad at me? It's complicated. I know I've messed up and haven't handled the situation very well."

Zach's attention zeroed in on her. "Billie, please tell me what's going on?"

She held Zach's penetrating gaze for a long moment, her lower lip trembling and her words choking in her throat. How could she explain what she'd done in a way that made sense?

"Billie," Wayne said, his voice gentle. "You have nothing to fear from me. Please believe that I've always had your best interests at heart."

She blinked multiple times, trying to keep her tears from escaping between her lashes. "I'm so sorry. I wish I could turn back the clock six months and do this the right way."

Zach's eyes widened. "Billie, why are you upset? What's wrong?"

She twisted her hands together in her lap. "Nothing's wrong, I've done something stupid."

Zach shook his head. "I don't get it. What could you have done that relates to Wayne?"

She met Zach's gaze, her tears threatening to stream out of her eyes. The moment of truth had arrived. "Wayne is my birth father."

Zach's jaw fell slack, Billie's quiet words registering in his mind. Wayne was Billie's birth father. How was that possible?

Billie placed her hand over his, her lower lip quivering. "I'm so sorry I didn't tell you earlier."

He shook off her hand. "You knew about this when we first met at Sapphire Bay?"

She nodded. "Please, Zach, I feel really bad and I can explain—"

"Explain what? That you've lied to me, and Wayne, for months?"

A couple of tears trickled down her face. "It's not like that. I had my reasons for staying quiet."

He clenched his fist under the table. "Your reasons? How can you justify not telling me something that's so important?"

Wayne cleared his throat. "Zach, it might be wise if you talk about this with Billie a bit later, before you both say things you might regret."

She pressed her fingertips on the corners of her eyes, blotting her tears. "I was planning to tell you everything this week, after your birthday."

Zach opened his wallet and slammed two fifty-dollar notes on the table. "That will cover our breakfast, and anything else you want." He stood. "I need some space."

Her face paled. "Where are you going?"

"I don't know. Somewhere. I need to think." His anger had built to a crescendo, threatening to push aside all rational thought. He had to get away from her, and try to calm down, gain some perspective.

"Please call me." Billie pressed her lips together. "I'm so sorry…"

He ignored Billie's plea and turned to Wayne. "I'm sorry she has deceived you, too. I hope you can work things out."

"Zach, I'm praying for you," Wayne said. "I know this news is a big shock and you need time to process it. I'll be in touch."

He nodded. "I've gotta go." He grabbed his jacket and strode out of the café, leaving his birthday gift from Billie on the table. The envelope would scorch his hands, a stark reminder of her deception. How could she act as if everything was normal and keep this huge secret from him?

Zach jogged along the street, heading in the direction of a cab rank. He could catch a cab home, grab his sailing gear and drive over to the yacht club. His yacht was his sanctuary, a place where he could get away from everything and be alone.

His phone buzzed and he ignored it. He'd already spoken with his parents this morning, and the rest of his family and friends had wished him happy birthday last night.

He shook his head. Last night he'd thought he was the luckiest man in the world. His future with Billie—his hopes and dreams for building a life and family with her—had seemed certain.

Now he felt lost, empty and disorientated. She'd dropped a bomb he'd never expected to hear. And on his birthday. Zach hailed a cab and arrived home within minutes. He settled the fare and raced indoors, anxious to escape to his yacht. Wayne was wise to suggest he take time out before talking with Billie. His simmering anger clouded his judgment.

In autopilot, he grabbed his gear and the picnic he'd prepared for them. His plans for a romantic day out on the water with Billie were decimated, a casualty of her revelation this morning.

He drove his SUV past Billie's apartment and his gut constricted, another wave of searing anger consuming him. Was Wayne the main reason she returned to church? Had she used him to get closer to Wayne?

A heavy stone lodged in his heart. Was this the only secret she hadn't shared? Could he expect to learn more bad news from the woman he loved?

Zach found a parking spot near the stairs leading down to the yacht club. He retrieved his dinghy from its home in the large boat shed, glad he hadn't run into anyone he knew well. A polite conversation about the weather and the prevailing winds was more than he could handle.

As he rowed out to his yacht, his muscles screamed as he powered the oars through the water. The pain hit him hard and he welcomed its sting, a panacea after the stressful events at the café. He reached his yacht, hooked up the ladder and climbed aboard.

The familiar movements calmed his blood pressure, the gentle swaying of the yacht and the tangy sea air restoring his equilibrium. He opened the hatch and stored his gear belowdeck.

The light breeze cooled his bare arms, the air too calm to fill the sails. He checked the fuel level before motoring around a couple of headlands and dropping anchor off an isolated cove that was inaccessible by road.

His phone beeped again and he ignored the messages on the screen, switching it to silent. Below deck he located his beaten-up Bible, the spine falling apart in his hands, and he threw a couple of cushions on a bench seat in the cockpit.

The cushions squeaked as he stretched out lengthwise on the bench seat. He opened his Bible to Psalm 46 and closed his eyes. *Please, Lord, give me Your peace and help me to discern the truth about Billie. Can I trust her?*

He shaded his eyes and read the faded text on wafer-thin pages. *God is our refuge and strength.* He meditated on verse one, the words seeping into his heart and mind.

Billie's decision to withhold important information had wounded him. He'd trusted her and he'd shared his life with her. He had refrained from discussing his ideas for attending Bible college, but they weren't a sure thing and he hadn't made a firm commitment.

He rubbed his hands over his eyes, his head starting to throb. He prayed that Billie and Wayne had managed to have a constructive conversation. He respected Wayne and appreciated that he was willing to embrace Billie in his life. Wayne wouldn't have offered her accommodation in his home, knowing she might be his daughter, if he'd planned to reject her.

Billie's intense sadness when she had talked about her birth mother's death lingered in his mind. He remembered their evening conversations on her deck at Sapphire Bay. Her cynicism regarding the integrity of church people was genuine. People had hurt her in the past. She had valid reasons for distrusting the church and hesitating at the thought of becoming a pastor's wife.

Zach finished reading the chapter and closed his eyes. Exhaustion from the party last night and the emotions from this morning had worn him out. He dragged his hat over his face and rested his head on the coarse cushion. The warmth from the sun and the rhythmic rolling of the yacht lured him into a midday slumber.

Chapter 15

Billie held Zach's birthday card, tracing her fingertips over the embossing on the pale blue envelope and willing away her tears. Zach had left the café in a rush, the card remaining on the table. Forgotten or unwanted?

Wayne sat across from her, worry lines prominent on his forehead. "Are you okay?"

She shook her head.

"Would you like another coffee? Something else to drink? I wouldn't mind a second cappuccino."

"Yes, please. A cappuccino would be nice."

Wayne signaled a waiter, rolled up the fifty-dollar notes Zach had tossed on the table and tucked them in his top shirt pocket. "I'll settle the bill when we leave. I'm not in a rush if you're happy to talk."

She blinked, her eyes watery. "Thank you for not hating me."

He drew his eyebrows into a straight line. "I could never hate you. You're my daughter, my only daughter."

Her breathing settled back into a regular rhythm. "How long have you known?"

"I didn't know for sure until last night. A month ago I attended a church leaders meeting in the city and visited with your grandparents. They live in Birchgrove, not far from the wharf on the western side of the city. I sometimes stay with them."

Her eyes widened. "Are you talking about my birth mother's parents? They're alive and in Sydney?"

"Yes, they're very much alive and active for their age."

"Wow. I had no idea and I couldn't find any information on their whereabouts."

"Did you know they migrated here?"

She shook her head. "I knew they were living overseas around the time my birth mother passed."

"Billie, I'm so sorry I wasn't here to comfort you when you learned that news. Her death was a shock to all of us, a sudden accident that your grandparents have struggled to cope with. I started to connect the dots when your grandmother showed me old photos of Anna, your mother. You bear a striking resemblance to her."

"Really?"

"Yes. I don't know how I didn't notice it before. Zach had mentioned you were adopted, which had stayed in my mind because I'd always hoped to reconnect with you one day. Your grandparents, and my wife and I, have prayed we'd meet you."

She swiped at the fresh tears forming in her eyes, her heart overwhelmed by the genuine caring from this man. Her birth father.

"Your wife is okay with all this? Do the boys know about me?"

He sighed. "We've always been open and honest with the boys. I was only nineteen when I dated Anna at university. We both studied teaching, although Anna was always a free spirit who dreamed of traveling the world."

A waiter placed two cappuccinos on their table.

She stirred in a sachet of raw sugar, the crystals melting in the milky froth as she absorbed his words.

"Billie, I wasn't a Christian at the time. My father has always hated the church, and religion in general. My parents were quite liberal in their views when I was growing up and I didn't have a strong moral compass."

"What about Anna? Did she believe in God?"

He nodded. "She had faith but rebelled against the rules of her childhood church after she left school. I wanted to marry her when we found out she was pregnant."

She lifted her brow. "That's a big commitment to make when you were so young."

"Yes. I cared for your mother and I had thought we were in love. But, she didn't believe she could settle down and become a good Italian wife and mother—her parents' expectation. Adoption was the heartbreaking but logical answer."

He sipped his cappuccino, his voice choking up as he continued. "I was devastated and our romantic relationship ended before you were born. Losing you was the catalyst for me to start searching for meaning in my life. I was invited to a Christian group on campus and my faith developed from there."

She dabbed her eyes with a napkin, goose bumps forming on her arms. "What an incredible testimony."

"It gets better. I met my wife at church a few years later, during my first year of teaching, and we married within a year. Kirsty is the love of my life."

"Like a fairy tale. What happened to Anna? Was she happy?"

He shrugged. "It's hard to know. She moved to Italy not long after you were born and I stayed in touch with your grandparents. They struggled for years to forgive Anna for rejecting my marriage proposal and letting you go."

"Was she their only child?"

"Yes, and their only living relative in Australia. They're retired now and travel to Europe every second year to see their family. Your grandfather was very hardworking, and owned a profitable convenience store for many years."

"Why didn't you all search for me, if you were praying for a reunion?"

He let out a sharp breath. "It wasn't our choice. Anna was adamant that she didn't want us to seek you out and disrupt your life. She assumed you'd be happy with your adopted family and might not want to know us."

She bit her lip. "Would she have rejected me?"

"No, don't ever think that. She always said she'd welcome you with open arms if you chose to find her."

"Are both of your parents still alive? Do you have siblings?"

He nodded. "I have two younger sisters and a brother who live in Sydney with their families. My parents are in their late seventies and are struggling with a few health issues. The whole extended family know of your existence, and I promise they'll welcome you into the family. As will your maternal grandparents."

She met his warm gaze. "I'm stunned and I don't know what to say. I had feared being rejected by you, knowing you're a pastor."

He shook his head. "I'm not ashamed of you. If people want to judge me, so be it. It's God's opinion that matters, not the opinion of others."

"I agree." She finished her cappuccino, her heart overflowing with gratitude. *Thank you, Lord.*

"Billie, I've loved you since you were a tiny babe I held in my arms for only a few minutes."

She parted her lips, stunned by his words. "You were there when I was born?"

"I was at the hospital, and we took a few photos of you before we let you go." He blinked, his eyes welling with tears. "Believe me, that was the hardest day of my life.

Handing you back to the midwife and knowing I may never see you again. But God is good. He blessed you with a wonderful adopted family and blessed us with the opportunity to reconnect today."

"We are blessed. If only Zach was here with me."

He patted her hand. "Don't worry, I suspect he has headed out on his yacht by himself to calm down and think. I'll message him now, and wait for him at the yacht club if necessary. I promise I'll do my best to help him understand why you kept quiet."

"Thank you." Her lower lip trembled. "I didn't tell anyone, not even my sister. I'm praying he'll listen and forgive me."

"Zach is a reasonable man and his pride is hurt. Give him time to process everything and he'll come around. I know he loves you, which is why he's feeling hurt and betrayed."

"I love him, too." But was her love sufficient? Could he surrender his anger and restore his trust in her? She'd do whatever it took to reconcile with him and reestablish their relationship on a solid foundation of complete honesty.

Zach woke from a deep sleep, disorientated and restless. The yacht rocked beneath him and the scratchy cushions dug into his bare legs. He sat up, in a daze as he recalled the events of this morning. Billie owed him an explanation. He'd listen to her side of the story before casting judgment or blame.

He switched on his phone, scanning his messages. Two from Billie and five from Wayne. He opened Wayne's most recent message, sent only five minutes ago. Wayne was on his way to the yacht club from Manly, alone and wanting to talk.

Zach rolled his shoulders, loosening the tension knots

that had formed while he slept. He replied to Wayne's message, arranging to meet outside the yacht club. If he pulled up anchor now, he should make it back to his mooring before Wayne arrived. Sunday afternoon traffic over the Spit Bridge would make Wayne's journey longer than he probably anticipated.

He grabbed a couple of sandwiches and a bottle of water from belowdeck before switching on the engine. The breeze had picked up, but it was faster to motor back to the bay. Before long he'd eaten his lunch, steered his boat into the mooring, packed up and rowed into shore. He stored his dinghy in the shed and gathered up all his bags.

Wayne stood outside the entrance to the yacht club, his expression serious. Zach hoped and prayed Wayne and Billie had parted on good terms.

He walked over to Wayne. "Hey, thanks for coming here to see me."

Wayne nodded. "Have you had a chance to think and pray?"

"Yes, and I fell asleep on the boat while I was praying."

"The sleep probably did you the world of good, after staying up late last night. Is there somewhere we can talk?"

"We can go inside. There's tea and coffee there, too."

"Perfect."

Wayne followed him into a spacious room overlooking the harbor. Zach stashed his gear in a corner and pulled out a chair at the closest table by the window. The room was nearly empty. Two elderly men were talking in the far corner.

"Would you like tea or coffee? I have cookies in one of my bags, if you're hungry."

"Tea will be fine. I had lunch with Billie not long ago."

Zach paused. "You spent the whole morning with her?"

"Yes, and she's planning to stay with us for the weekend in Riverwood in a couple of weeks. I hope you can join us."

Wayne's question hung in the air and Zach drew in a deep breath. "I'd like that, if things work out between me and Billie."

"Billie's a great girl, and I'm not just saying that because she's my daughter. She loves you and she wants to make things right in your relationship."

Zach stood at the counter near their table, preparing two mugs of hot tea. "I still don't get why she couldn't tell me the truth. It makes me wonder if she's hiding other stuff from me."

Wayne sighed. "My job was the problem and her big stumbling block. Her bad experiences with church people meant she didn't know if she could trust me. It would be a no-brainer for my father, her grandfather, to understand her logic. My old man would probably applaud her skepticism. I suspect those two will get along well."

"What do you mean?" He placed a mug in front of Wayne and sat in the chair opposite, sipping his tea.

"My father assumes all church people, especially pastors, are hypocrites and are horrible people until they prove to him otherwise. Billie was concerned I'd be embarrassed or ashamed of her existence, and want to keep it a secret."

He nodded. "You're talking about the social stigma in church circles."

"Absolutely. I wasn't a Christian when she was born. The truth is giving Billie up for adoption was a catalyst for me to explore faith matters. But, she didn't know the circumstances, and didn't know that I'd never considered her an indiscretion I'd rather forget. From my years in ministry, I know that many adoption reunions aren't positive experiences."

Zach leaned forward in his seat, cradling his cup in both

hands. "How did your father cope with your decision to become a pastor?"

"Not well. Twenty years later and he still has a big problem with it. I pray that his heart will soften, but that's up to God. I can't force my father to approve of my vocation."

"That's not easy."

"Life isn't easy." Wayne sipped his tea. "Have you made a decision about your future career direction?"

He shook his head. "A year ago it all made sense. Bible college next year when I was debt-free, owned the apartment outright and had consolidated my investments. Now, I'm not so sure."

"Because of Billie."

"I love her and I know she's not keen on the idea of becoming a pastor's wife."

"She might have a change of heart."

"It's not fair to assume she'll change her mind. If I ask her to marry me, I need to be prepared to let go of that dream and pray for an opportunity to arise that works for both of us."

"You have given this a lot of thought and prayer."

Zach placed his empty cup on the table. "I've scoured the Bible in search of answers, reading many of the Old Testament stories. I'm trusting that God will show me the right path, rather than assuming that I know what's best."

Wayne nodded. "I'll continue praying for you—and praying that I'll become one of your fathers-in-law sooner rather than later."

He smiled. "Thank you. I need to reply to Billie's messages."

"Will you see her today?"

"I hope so, and I'll try to end my birthday on a high note. Today has not worked out the way I'd planned."

"My timing, in terms of approaching Billie with my suspicions, wasn't helpful."

Zach shrugged. "The truth had to come out eventually." He fished his phone out of his pocket and typed in a message for Billie. The sooner he had a chance to sit down and talk with her, the better. It was time to clear the air and see if they had a future together.

Later in the afternoon Billie pressed the buzzer at Zach's apartment, her stomach queasy. He'd sent her a message a few hours ago, asking if she'd meet him. She'd nearly suggested her apartment instead, now it was pristine after she'd spent the afternoon cleaning it from top to bottom. Her therapy time to ponder her long conversations with Wayne.

Zach buzzed her in and she opened the external door. Trepidation filled each step as she walked closer to the elevator. Soon she would learn if she had a future with Zach or a broken heart.

The elevator whizzed up to his level and she met Zach at his door.

His eyes drank in her appearance, as if he hadn't seen her for weeks. "Come in."

"Thanks." She strolled ahead and settled on her favorite sofa with a view of Manly Wharf.

He hovered in the entrance to his living room. "Would you like a drink? Something to eat? I was going to make a latte for myself."

"A latte would be nice."

"Okay, I'll be back soon."

She kicked off her sandals and tucked her feet under her body, the soft leather comfortable against her skin. *Lord, please help me to say the right words. I love Zach and I'm sorry I've hurt him. Please forgive me, and I pray Zach will forgive me.*

Minutes later he returned with their lattes on a small tray. Her fingers grazed his as he passed over the mug, the familiar jolt of awareness bringing a smile to her lips. "Thank you."

"You're welcome." He lowered his body onto the sofa beside her, leaving a foot of space between them.

She resisted the urge to wriggle closer and snuggle up next to him. First she needed to make things right between them. "I'm so sorry about everything."

He nodded. "I've had time to think and pray."

"I feel really bad that I've ruined your birthday."

He sipped his latte, his gaze focused on the harbor view. "Why couldn't you tell me the truth? Don't you trust me?"

She picked up the sugar bowl that lived on his coffee table and stirred a teaspoon of the fine granules into her latte.

She let out a small sigh. "The problem is me, not you. I messed up. You've never done anything to suggest you're untrustworthy."

"But you still didn't tell me."

She paused, her body rigid and her voice catching in her throat. "I couldn't bring myself to tell anyone, not even Julia."

He swung around to face her. "I thought you told her everything."

She shook her head and sucked the frothy milk off her teaspoon. "I tend to be a bit of a loner, which is why I loved being by myself at the beach house. I have friends I do stuff with but I'm not good at sharing my deepest thoughts and feelings, not even with my sister."

He tipped his head to the side and rested his arm along the back of the sofa. "I thought you were very open with me right from the start. We talked for hours on your deck at the beach house."

"Zach, I'm different around you. I can talk to you about the things that matter and know you won't judge me. I haven't shared the stuff I told you in Sapphire Bay about my birth mom with anyone else."

He nodded. "If that's true, then why did you hold back on telling me about Wayne? Were you afraid of my reaction?"

She chewed on the inside of her cheek, her lashes lowered. "It was too raw and painful to articulate in words. I was petrified Wayne would reject me and break my heart. I'd known too many church people who cared more about their image and maintaining appearances than about the truth or people's feelings. And once I told you, I knew I'd have to approach Wayne. I wasn't ready."

"My mom also shares your feelings about the church."

"I really respect your mom for not allowing her prejudices to discourage you and your sisters from attending church." She drank her latte, needing a sweet dose of courage as she met his gaze. "I nearly fell apart and burst into tears at the café in Riverwood when Wayne stopped by our table. I had started to get to know him as a person and new doubts had crept into my mind. I kept wondering if I was wrong to question whether Wayne was a decent person who would accept me."

He sipped his coffee, his gaze remaining on her face. "From the start you'd assumed that Wayne would reject you?"

"Yes, pretty much."

"Why did you bother going to Sapphire Bay?"

She groaned and leaned forward, putting her half-empty mug on the coffee table. "You'll think I'm crazy. My plan had been to check him out from afar, visit his church a couple of times and keep a low profile in town by hiding out in Sapphire Bay. If he seemed okay, I'd contact him through official channels when I returned to Sydney."

"Wow, you had it all mapped out."

"Except God had other plans that also involved you."

His lips twitched into a wry smile. "God has a habit of doing that and turning our plans upside down."

She nodded. "I didn't factor in being drawn back to church and my faith strengthening through Wayne's sermons and meeting you. Then I hit Wayne's radar, which made everything more messy and complicated. The deception became too real and I feared the consequences when the truth was finally revealed."

He finished his latte and placed his mug on the table. "I'm glad I had a chance to calm down before we talked."

"Thank you for listening to my story. You now know all my faults."

"Billie, I believe you, and I believe that you didn't intend to hurt anyone. I knew you weren't comfortable in church and I held back on telling you about my Bible college plans. I'm not perfect and I've made my share of mistakes. Making assumptions and not giving you the benefit of the doubt this morning is one of them."

"I understand why you were angry."

"I was hurt and I needed to work out what to do next."

She twisted her hands together in her lap, digging her nails into her palms. It was now or never. Time to learn her fate. "Can you forgive me?"

Chapter 16

Zach's heart constricted, his love for Billie overflowing in response to her honest and earnest question. "I forgive you."

Her eyes shimmered in the soft afternoon sunlight. "Thank you. It means a lot to me."

He held her hand, tracing his fingertips over her smooth palm. "You mean a lot to me."

"Can we wipe the slate clean, and start over?"

"I'd like that. But first, tell me how things went with Wayne. Are you happy?"

Her mouth curved into a vivacious smile. "Yes, he is so understanding. And he told me the whole story."

As Billie shared her conversations with Wayne, Zach listened with pleasure. Something had shifted in Billie and she seemed so free and light, a burden lifted.

"Billie, you know what this means? He always wanted you and he never rejected you."

"I know. I'm still very emotional and astounded when I think about how he has faithfully prayed for me for years."

"God was looking after you, even when you felt like you were alone and in the wilderness."

"I understand that now. I agreed to visit Wayne in a couple of weeks and meet his family in Riverwood."

"Will your parents be home by then?"

She nodded. "They're flying home earlier than planned, and will be back in Sydney in five days time."

He tucked a lock of hair behind her ear, his hand lingering on her cheek. "Billie, I love you and I want to explore a future with you, if you'll have me?"

Her eyes softened. "I love you, and I didn't know if you'd be prepared to give me another chance."

He tipped up her chin, depositing a firm kiss on her parted lips. "Can I come to Riverwood with you?"

"Of course." She scooted closer and wrapped her arms around him, tucking her head under his chin. "I want you there with me, supporting me, when I officially meet Wayne's family."

He stroked her hair, inhaling the light floral fragrance of her shampoo. "Have you told your parents or Julia about Wayne?"

"Not yet. Julia will be thrilled but I'd rather tell my mom and dad in person. I'll wait until they return before I say anything to my sister."

"Good idea. How do you think your parents will cope with your news?"

"Dad should be fine but my mom is quite sensitive. It may take her some time to adjust to the news. She was very upset when I told her my birth mother had passed away."

"Understandable. Your family will have to adjust to the changes, now you've gained a whole new family."

"And four grandparents. Hard to believe." She wriggled in his arms, a quiver entering her voice. "I look forward to the day I can meet my maternal grandparents and learn more about my birth mother. I thought that information was lost to me forever. But, I have a question for you. Do you still want to be a pastor?"

He paused, her question cementing his new decision

in his mind. "Maybe, maybe not. I don't know how long I can continue working crazy hours in my current job and I'd like to have more time to spend with you."

"I like the sound of that."

He splayed his hand on her trim waist. "The thing is, I don't know if becoming a pastor is what I really want to do with my life. It's still an option, but I can see myself being fulfilled doing something else. There are many different ways we can serve God."

"True. We can pray about it."

"Definitely." He closed his eyes, content to hold her close in his arms, her head resting against his heart. *Thank you, Lord, for bringing Billie into my life.*

Two weeks later, Billie walked hand in hand along Sapphire Bay Beach with Zach. The Sunday afternoon beach crowd had thinned out as they strolled along the soft sand toward her old beach house. Who lived in the beach house now? Would the occupants be sitting on the back deck, enjoying the unseasonably warm sunshine?

Zach squeezed her hand. "How are you feeling?"

"Blessed." She smiled, her heart light. "It's so good to be back here, kind of like coming home."

"You now have family to visit here, so it's like your second home."

"True. I'm feeling very loved. Wayne's family was so sweet, and not at all put off by the fact I'd kept my identity hidden."

"I presume Wayne has paved the way for you, providing an explanation that must have satisfied their curiosity."

"I guess so." She quickened her pace as they reached the firm sand closer to the water's edge. "Everything he says makes this easier for me."

"He really has embraced you as his daughter."

"I know. I'm curious about the surprise he has planned for tonight."

Zach shortened his stride, falling into sync with her. "Possibly a family dinner? We had our reunion with the congregation from Riverwood at church this morning."

"I'm glad it's a holiday weekend and we can stay until tomorrow."

"And next weekend we're doing the bridge climb."

"I'm so excited."

Zach grinned. "You'll have to wake up early. I'll be knocking on your door at four in the morning, and you'd better be ready."

"I promise I'll wake up in time." The husband of one of her friends at work had proposed to her friend on the Sydney Harbour Bridge during their climb. Billie's heart skittered to a faster rhythm. Did Zach have plans to ask her to marry him next weekend?

She let out a wistful sigh. "Oh, there's my house."

Zach laughed. "Technically, it's not your house anymore."

"I know, but I still feel attached to it. Maybe it's because we met and got to know each other there."

"Our holiday romance that neither of us planned."

"But I'm glad it happened. We met at the right time, in the right place."

She let go of his hand and jogged up to the back gate. "It looks empty. There's no furniture on the deck anymore."

"Do you want to go into the backyard and take a closer look?"

"Zach, we can't do that!"

He shrugged. "I don't think anyone is home."

"But we'd be trespassing on private property."

"Aren't you just a little bit curious? The view from the

deck is much better than from here, and the neighbors can't see in over the fences."

"I can't believe you're encouraging me to do the wrong thing."

His eyes sparkled. "All right, what if I confessed that we have permission?"

"How? Do you know the owner?"

"I sure do." He pulled on the handle, opening the unlocked gate. "After you."

She walked barefoot over the grass and climbed the flight of stairs to the deck. The house looked unoccupied, the blinds drawn over the windows. "I miss this house."

"I know." He held her hand and bent down on one knee.

She gasped, her eyes moist. "Oh Zach, I can't believe it. It's really happening."

"Yes, when you give me a chance to ask the question."

She giggled. "Okay, I'll be quiet."

His eyes gleamed and a big smile covered his face, his dimple appearing on his cheek. "Billie, you are the most incredible woman I've ever met. Beautiful, intelligent, thoughtful. I love you and I would love to spend the rest of my life with you."

He pulled a small red velvet box out of his pocket and flipped the lid open. A brilliant ruby ring set with smaller diamonds twinkled in the sunlight. "Billie, will you marry me?"

Her heart swelled. "Yes, yes. Zach, I love you more than I ever dreamed possible. I'd be honored to become your wife and spend the rest of my life with you."

He slipped the ring on her finger, a perfect fit.

"Wow, the ring is exquisite. I love the white gold setting."

He stood. "I'm glad you love it."

"I love you more." She threw her arms around his neck,

burying her face against his muscular chest. His heart rate accelerated and she let out a contented sigh.

"I have another surprise. Are you ready?"

She stepped back, tipping her head up and staring into his magnetic eyes. "What could match your proposal?"

He let go of her hand and retrieved something from his pocket. "How about this?" He opened his hand, revealing a set of keys.

"They look like house keys."

"Yes, a brand new set of keys for the beach house."

"But why do you have the keys?" She widened her eyes, the full implication of his words hitting her like a tsunami. "Did you buy the beach house?"

He grinned. "My wedding gift for you, if you want it?"

She opened her mouth, her words stuck somewhere in her throat for a long moment. "I don't know what to say."

"Wow, I never thought I'd render you speechless a second time."

She gave him a playful punch. "I'm in shock. I love this house and I love that you bought it for me. This house is expensive. What about Bible college?"

"It's a good investment and, when I approached the owners, I learned they had been thinking about selling. It was a win-win for everyone." He hadn't answered her question, but she let it go. She trusted him and whatever plans he made.

"Do you plan on renting it out to strangers?"

He shook his head. "Our family and friends can holiday here, when we're not visiting. I have it all sorted. Now, why don't you open the door to your new house?"

She jiggled the keys, unlocking the main sliding door and pushing aside the curtain. A table for two was set, refreshments laid out on a white linen tablecloth. "Oh Zach, you've thought of everything."

"Wayne was very helpful."

"He knows about the proposal?"

"Both of your fathers have given me their permission."

She laughed. "I'm still getting used to the idea of having two fathers."

"As long as you only want one husband."

"Yes, one husband for life is enough for me." She stood on her tiptoes and kissed her fiancé, hoping he would agree to a short engagement. Today couldn't possibly get any better.

A few hours later Billie walked up the front path of Wayne's home. Zach held her close, his arm draped around her shoulders. She lifted her left hand in the air, unable to keep her eyes off her engagement ring.

Zach rang the doorbell. "Are you ready to announce our news?"

"I can't wait."

The door opened. Wayne glanced at her ring and enfolded her in a warm hug. "Congratulations, I'm so happy for both of you."

Wayne gave Zach a brief hug and patted him on the back. "Well done and welcome to the family."

"Thank you. We appreciate your help today at the house."

Wayne smiled. "My pleasure. Let's head out the back. I know Kirsty and the boys are around somewhere."

She held Zach's hand and walked along the hall. The house was quiet, and she wondered if the boys had gone out. They entered the darkened family room, the curtains drawn. A light flicked on.

"Surprise!" A few dozen excited voices spoke in unison.

Billie gulped, placing her left hand over her mouth.

"Wow, all our family is here." She turned to Zach, her vision misty. "Did you know about this?"

He shook his head. "It's a big surprise for me, too."

Her parents hugged and kissed her, thrilled to celebrate their engagement. Julia and Sean were next with Zach's parents and sisters, congratulating them on their exciting news.

Kirsty embraced her in a long hug. "I hope you don't mind that we organized a surprise celebration tonight."

Billie shook her head. "It's lovely, thank you."

Kirsty flicked a few dark curls off her face. "When Zach shared his plans, we thought it would be nice for all of your family to be here to celebrate."

Billie nodded. "We really appreciate your warm welcome and everything you've done for us."

Wayne and Kirsty's boys each gave her an obligatory hug before shifting their full attention to Zach. It seemed like their new future brother-in-law was a welcome addition to their tribe.

Wayne moved to her side. "I'd like to introduce you and Zach to a couple of people who are thrilled to be here."

Zach entwined his fingers with hers. "Who are they? I thought I knew everyone here."

An elderly couple stepped forward, holding hands. Their bright eyes, dark brown like her own, held a shimmer of unshed tears.

Wayne cleared his throat, his voice hoarse. "Billie, I'm delighted to introduce you to your maternal grandparents."

Tears flowed down Billie's face as her gaze moved between their eager faces. "Wow, I'm so glad you could both be here."

Her grandmother held her close. "Please call me Nonna, and this is your nonno."

"You are so like our beautiful Anna." Her grandfather wiped at his eyes. "It's like she has returned to us."

Billie hugged and kissed her nonno, her mind spinning.

Her nonna held her hand, her gaze intense. "Your resemblance to our Anna is strong. We have prayed this day would come, when we'd be reunited with Anna's baby girl."

Billie grasped her grandparent's hands, her glassy eyes blurring her vision. "I wasn't expecting to see you so soon. I have so many questions about my mother and my heritage."

Her nonno nodded. "We can visit you in Sydney, or you can visit us. Anna would be so proud of you."

She held back a sob, her heart breaking anew over her loss. "I wish I'd had an opportunity to meet her and know her."

"We pray you will be reunited in eternity." Her Nonna blinked away her tears, her solemn face betraying her grief. "Our Anna was a headstrong girl. But, we believe she had faith and is with our heavenly father now."

Billie clutched their hands, her heart full to the brim with love for her family. "I hope we can see each other often."

Zach stood behind her, wrapping his arms around her and leaning close to her ear. "I love you, my precious girl."

She let go of her grandparents' hands and pressed a kiss on his cheek, seeking comfort in the arms of her soon-to-be husband.

Minutes later her mother and Zach's mother stood beside her grandparents, looking like they were on an important mission.

Zach's mom smiled. "Have you two lovebirds set a date?"

Billie giggled, happy tears threatening to flow from her moistened eyes. "Is before Christmas too soon?"

"Not at all," Zach said. "The sooner, the better, if you want my opinion."

Karen clucked and turned to Billie's mother. "It looks like we need to get moving with the engagement party plans. We can start tonight, after dinner."

Billie turned around in Zach's arms, meeting his gaze. "Now the fun begins."

He kissed the tip of her nose. "But it's worth it and I can't wait for you to be my bride."

Chapter 17

Six months later Billie waited at the side entrance to Beachside Community Church in her sleeveless silk-and-lace wedding gown. Julia adjusted her long veil and train.

Delicate lace and beading covered the bodice, the floor-length skirt floating around her legs. It was a warm afternoon and she was glad she had chosen to wear her hair up. Zach could have the fun job of helping her remove the dozens of hairpins later tonight.

Julia grinned, standing beside her for another photo. "You look beautiful, as always. I'm so proud to be your matron of honor."

"I'm happy you're here with me."

Julia and Zach's sisters wore vibrant long red bridesmaid dresses in a style similar to her own bridal gown. A few minutes earlier she'd caught a glimpse of Gus and Sean, dressed in their finery, at the back of the church. Their pastor friend Simon and her eldest half brother, Dan, waited with them inside the church with Zach.

Julia twisted a loose curl around her finger. "I'm looking forward to seeing Zach's face when you walk down the aisle."

She tightened her grip on her bridal bouquet of white and red roses. "I can't wait to see him."

Her adopted father moved to her side, his smile bright. "Billie, it's nearly time. Are you ready?"

She nodded. The tempo of the music inside the church transitioned into the traditional "Bridal Chorus." Bek walked ahead to the main center aisle, followed by Kelly, Mel and Julia.

Billie stepped forward with her father, thankful she'd chosen to wear comfortable, low heeled shoes. Cameras flashed as the congregation came into view and the photographer positioned them for more photos inside the church.

She walked down the center aisle on her father's arm, her gaze locking with Zach's. He stood tall and proud at the front of the church in his dark tuxedo and red bow tie, a brilliant smile on his handsome face.

She glanced at their guests lining the aisle, the familiar smiling faces of family and friends. Ryan stood close behind Cassie, his arms circling his wife's waist. The girls from work gathered in one row, their phones working overtime as they snapped photos.

Billie's gaze reached the front rows, her heart swelling as her nonna gave her a special smile. Last month her nonna had given her a precious pearl bracelet, a treasured jewel originally owned by Anna.

Billie's fingertips skimmed over the pearls surrounding her wrist as she held her heavy bouquet in place, delighted to be wearing something old from her birth mother. The bracelet was a perfect fit, and her mother had given her a matching set of earrings and a necklace.

Her mom smiled, unshed tears shimmering in her eyes.

She loved her parents and couldn't imagine growing up in a different family. Her parents had embraced Billie's new family into their lives. Wayne, Kirsty and the boys were staying with her parents for the weekend.

Wayne stood at the front, ready to officiate her wedding service. He gave her an encouraging smile, his gaze warm.

Billie nodded and gripped her father's arm, pleased he

was by her side. She'd never questioned his love for her, as strong as if she were his own flesh and blood.

Finally she reached Zach's side, his eyes glittering in the afternoon sunlight streaming through the stained glass windows.

Zach whispered in her ear, his breath tickling her neck. "You look incredible, my beautiful girl."

"Thank you, so do you." Billie held Zach's hand and stepped up on the stage, her pulse speeding up.

Wayne's smooth voice filled the church. Her father gave his permission for the marriage and stepped down to sit in the front row beside her mother.

The service passed quickly, her mind distracted by the man standing by her side. They had a long honeymoon planned. Skiing in Aspen first, followed by a few days in San Francisco and five days in Hawaii.

They'd spend two weeks back in Sydney before driving to Sapphire Bay to stay in their beach house over Christmas. A big family Christmas celebration was planned with her family and Zach's.

Billie stood opposite Zach, staring up into his luminous eyes. She repeated her vows in a strong voice, her promises before God, family and friends to love, honor and cherish her husband.

Zach's voice was deep and full of emotion, his loving words stirring her heart.

At Wayne's pronouncement, Zach lifted her sheer veil back off her face and lowered his head, his lips seeking a response.

She deepened the kiss and wrapped her arms around his neck, her mind suspended in time as a torrent of feelings washed over her.

Loud clapping from the congregation drew her back to reality and she opened her eyes.

Zach chuckled, his voice low. "We can continue this later."

Her hand lingered on the side of his face. "I'm looking forward to it."

They signed their marriage certificate with Julia and Gus as their witnesses.

As they walked up the aisle she leaned close to Zach. "We did it."

He grinned. "I'm blessed to have you as my wife."

Her cheeks warmed. "We're both blessed to have a new life together." Her search for her birth father had yielded more than she'd ever dreamed possible. God brought Zach into her life and gave her beautiful relationships with her birth family. She couldn't wait for the next chapter of her life to begin.

* * * * *

REQUEST YOUR FREE BOOKS!

2 FREE INSPIRATIONAL NOVELS
PLUS 2
FREE
MYSTERY GIFTS

Love Inspired®

YES! Please send me 2 FREE Love Inspired® novels and my 2 FREE mystery gifts (gifts are worth about $10). After receiving them, if I don't wish to receive any more books, I can return the shipping statement marked "cancel." If I don't cancel, I will receive 6 brand-new novels every month and be billed just $4.99 per book in the U.S. or $5.49 per book in Canada. That's a saving of at least 17% off the cover price. It's quite a bargain! Shipping and handling is just 50¢ per book in the U.S. and 75¢ per book in Canada.* I understand that accepting the 2 free books and gifts places me under no obligation to buy anything. I can always return a shipment and cancel at any time. Even if I never buy another book, the two free books and gifts are mine to keep forever.

105/305 IDN GH5P

Name	(PLEASE PRINT)	
Address		Apt. #
City	State/Prov.	Zip/Postal Code

Signature (if under 18, a parent or guardian must sign)

Mail to the **Reader Service:**
IN U.S.A.: P.O. Box 1867, Buffalo, NY 14240-1867
IN CANADA: P.O. Box 609, Fort Erie, Ontario L2A 5X3

**Are you a subscriber to Love Inspired® books
and want to receive the larger-print edition?
Call 1-800-873-8635 or visit www.ReaderService.com.**

* Terms and prices subject to change without notice. Prices do not include applicable taxes. Sales tax applicable in N.Y. Canadian residents will be charged applicable taxes. Offer not valid in Quebec. This offer is limited to one order per household. Not valid for current subscribers to Love Inspired books. All orders subject to credit approval. Credit or debit balances in a customer's account(s) may be offset by any other outstanding balance owed by or to the customer. Please allow 4 to 6 weeks for delivery. Offer available while quantities last.

Your Privacy—The Reader Service is committed to protecting your privacy. Our Privacy Policy is available online at www.ReaderService.com or upon request from the Reader Service.

We make a portion of our mailing list available to reputable third parties that offer products we believe may interest you. If you prefer that we not exchange your name with third parties, or if you wish to clarify or modify your communication preferences, please visit us at www.ReaderService.com/consumerschoice or write to us at Reader Service Preference Service, P.O. Box 9062, Buffalo, NY 14240-9062. Include your complete name and address.

LI15